The Shakespeare Plot
Book 3

The Powder Treason

Alex Woolf

SCRIBO
a SALARIYA *imprint*

First published in Great Britain by Scribo MMXVIII
Scribo, a division of Book House, an imprint of
The Salariya Book Company
25 Marlborough Place, Brighton, BN1 1UB
www.salariya.com

ISBN 978-1-912006-33-5

The right of Alex Woolf to be identified as the author of this work has been asserted
in accordance with sections 77 and 78 of the Copyright, Designs
and Patents Act, 1988.

Book Design by David Salariya

Condition of Sale

Printed and bound in China

The text for this book is set in Cochin
The display type is P22 Operina

www.salariya.com

The Shakespeare Plot
Book 3

The Powder Treason

Alex Woolf

SCRIBO

a SALARIYA *imprint*

'What's Macbeth about, Mr Shakespeare?'
asked Alice.

'The perils of ambition,' answered Will. 'A general called Macbeth receives a prophecy from three witches that one day he'll be king of Scotland. Driven by ambition and urged on by his wife, he kills King Duncan and seizes the throne. Of course it all ends in tyranny, madness and death for Macbeth. Richard Burbage should have a lot of fun with the role.'

Act One

Chapter 1

The Warehouse

PORT OF LONDON, 30TH OCTOBER 1605

Tom Cavendish crouched in the shadows behind a pillar in the old warehouse, watching. A few yards away, near the warehouse entrance, two men were heaving barrels onto the back of a waiting cart. Tom had to be extremely quiet and still. It was vital that neither of the men knew they were being observed. One of the men was small and thin, and struggled to lift his end of each barrel. The other was taller but just as slender, and Tom immediately identified him as the more dangerous of the two. He couldn't see him very well in the poor light, but what he did see made him nervous – something to do with the man's wiry build, gaunt face and long yellow teeth.

The double doors of the warehouse stood wide open, admitting a block of dusty sunlight, together with the usual sounds of the quayside – the creak of ships, the shouts of dockers and the grind of the treadwheel cranes. The Port of London, on the north bank of the Thames, was England's gateway to the world. The produce of faraway kingdoms and empires, after weeks on the high seas, all fetched up here in this warehouse and others along the bank. Inside these crates and barrels was glassware from Venice, olive oil and dried fruit from Spain, furs from Russia, tobacco from the West Indies, cotton from Africa, silk from Persia, porcelain from China and spices from the East Indies. He could smell the sweet, woody aroma of nutmeg. Tom recognised it because his master, Sir Francis Bacon, insisted on using this luxury spice to season his pastries.

Right now, the thought of serving up a nutmeg-seasoned pastry to Sir Francis in his library was very comforting. He would prefer to be doing that than squatting here in the cold shadows, squashed uncomfortably between a pillar and a coil of heavy iron chains stacked against the wall.

Sometimes, after Tom had served Sir Francis his snack, he would invite Tom, unless he was very busy, to tarry a while and talk (Tom was never too busy to decline an invitation to tarry in Sir Francis's company). His master would go to one of the shelves of his vast library and take down a volume by someone like Thomas Aquinas or William of Ockham, and he would read out a passage. Then he would pose a question arising from this, which Tom would try to answer as best he could, and this would result in a conversation, which could last for an hour or more.

It was unusual for a serving boy to be treated by his master like this, almost as an equal, but then Tom was not typical. From the moment they met, Sir Francis had recognised in Tom someone who shared his curiosity about the world. He also knew that he would never have complete authority over him in the way that masters traditionally had over their servants. He had to share him with another far more powerful person. Namely, the king. For Tom had another job – a very secret job. When he wasn't working for Sir Francis Bacon, he was working as a spy in the service of England. And this was how he came to be crouching here in a cold, dusty warehouse watching two unsavoury characters heaving barrels onto a cart.

That morning, Tom had been summoned to Whitehall Palace to see Lord Robert Cecil, the king's spymaster. Cecil made these summonses from time to time. It was always unexpected, always urgent, and Tom was obliged to drop everything and come at once, no matter what he was doing. Sir Francis never complained. In his words, 'My needs can wait, Tom. The king's cannot.'

A shipment of French wine had arrived at the Port of London the previous evening, Cecil explained to Tom when he arrived. There was nothing unusual about that, of course. French wine was arriving in London all the time. But an eagle-eyed customs official had noticed an irregularity in the paperwork, which he'd brought to Cecil's attention. This led Cecil to suspect that the wine in the barrels might be illegal. In other words, the exporters had not paid the customs duties payable by all those who wished to trade with England.

Most administrators, when faced with a case like this, would simply move in and arrest the smugglers and force them to pay what was owed, plus a hefty fine – but not Cecil. For Cecil reckoned there might be something deeper and darker going on. This illegal wine, so his theory went, had been brought here to be sold to raise money for *nefarious purposes*. When Cecil said *nefarious purposes*, what he really meant was 'a papist plot'. In other words, a Catholic plot to overthrow the king of England.

This would be quite an extraordinary leap of logic for most people, though not for Cecil. For he was the sort of person who saw Catholic plots *everywhere*. As a result, he had no difficulty in linking a cargo of dodgy wine with a conspiracy to topple the king. His fellow courtiers laughed at him. They called him the Beagle on account of his small size, but also because he was so dogged in his obsessions. The Beagle, so they claimed, would suspect a migrating bird of papist sympathies if that bird happened to winter in Catholic Spain. Yet even his sternest critics had to admit that for more than ten years, the Beagle had kept England safe.

'Discover the customer, Tom,' Cecil had instructed his young spy. 'Find out where the barrels are going. That way we'll be able to trace the link between the wine and the conspiracy.'

'There almost certainly isn't a conspiracy,' Tom had wanted to say. But he'd held his tongue because he feared and respected the Beagle far too much to argue with him. And now, several hours later, here he was, watching these men (who were almost certainly small-time smugglers and not papist plotters or anything of that sort) load the barrels onto the cart and wondering how the devil he was supposed to find out where they were going.

By now the eight large barrels had been loaded, and the cart was visibly sagging under their combined weight. The smaller of the men was busy tying a rope across the rear of the cart to secure the barrels in place. 'Where shall I take them, Mr Keyes?' he asked.

Keyes replied: 'Take them to Mr Roberts on Lower Marsh in Lambeth, go straight there, mind, no stopping for an ale at the tavern, for you'll need all your wits about you to navigate the roads down Lambeth way, them being highly treacherous, partikerly in the dark and the fog, and there's always fog in Lambeth, one slip and you're in the marsh, not that me or

Mr Roberts will shed too many tears about that, as it's the safety of the barrels what concerns us. You is expendable Mr Wright, but the barrels, they is not, they have to reach Mr Roberts in perfick condition, otherwise, even assuming you survive the marsh, you is not leaving Lambeth except in a coffin.'

Keyes spoke these words in a continuous stream without once drawing breath, and all the while keeping his eyes fixed like shiny grey pins on Mr Wright.

After listening to this speech, Tom thought: *I do not want to cross paths with this man. No way.* And no sooner had this thought flashed through his brain, than disaster struck…

Over the past few minutes, Tom's left leg had started cramping, and in an effort to get the blood flowing through it again, he shifted position. This caused the coil of chains he was leaning against to make an audible clinking sound. The two men immediately turned their heads in his direction. Tom froze.

'Is someone here, Mr Keyes?' murmured Wright.

Keyes didn't reply. He drew his sword and began clambering over sacks and boxes towards where Tom was hidden. Tom squeezed himself more tightly behind the pillar, trying to make himself as small as possible, keeping his head down in case Keyes glimpsed the whites of his eyes. He could hear the man blundering about in the darkness, kicking over urns and poking his sword into hessian sacks.

'Probably just a cat or a rat,' suggested Wright.

Keyes stopped moving then, and Tom prayed he'd given up – until he felt something sharp and cold pressing into the back of his neck: the tip of a sword.

'On yer feet, sonny boy,' growled Keyes.

Grimacing, Tom got up, keeping his back to the smuggler.

'Who are you?' Keyes demanded.

'No one.'

The sword tip nudged forwards, biting into Tom's skin.

'Answer me!' the man snarled.

'I'm a docker.'

'And why would a docker be sitting back here in the shadows spying on us?'

'I wasn't spying on you. I was… having a rest.'

Tom was taking advantage of the darkness to slowly draw his sword.

'I say you was spying on us.'

'You're wrong.'

'Who sent you?'

Tom suddenly whirled around and batted Keyes' sword away with his own. He'd hoped to smash it from his hand, but Keyes maintained his grip on the weapon. Desperate to maintain the advantage of surprise, Tom barged into the taller man's chest, causing him to stumble backwards. But before he could bring his sword to Keyes' throat, the smuggler slithered away, deeper into the shadows.

Tom peered around, trying to gauge where the man had got to. Then he heard the swish of Keyes' sword, followed by the crack of splintering wood and an ominous rumble. Acting on pure instinct, Tom dived to his left just as half a dozen heavy barrels rolled off a collapsing shelf and crashed to the floor where he'd been standing. Keyes had meant to crush him.

While Tom was still on his knees, a line of gleaming steel flashed out of the darkness towards his head. At the last second, he raised his sword and parried Keyes' blade. He could see the man's yellow-toothed leer as he tried to keep Tom pinned to the floor. Keyes pressed mercilessly downwards, crushing Tom's sword hilt against his chin. Tom rammed his knee into the man's ankle. Keyes staggered from this unexpected assault, and Tom was able to squirm out from beneath him and regain his feet. He leapt onto a box and aimed a sudden blow at Keyes' neck. Sparks flew as Keyes parried and then pushed back. Tom came at him again. Savagely they attacked each other, smashing sword against sword with all their strength, searching for a weak point in the other's defence.

Tom had a height advantage, thanks to the box. He'd also been trained well, first by Sir John Davies at Essex House, and more recently by Robert Armin of the King's Men, who was giving him weekly lessons paid for by Lord Cecil. He knew the importance of posture, balance and lightness of feet. He knew how to keep his blade close and his movements firm yet controlled so as not to expose himself to counter-attacks. His disciplined style seemed to anger his adversary who was becoming increasingly wild in his swings and thrusts. Tom stayed calm, waiting for his opportunity. When Keyes was late to a block, Tom's sword tip sliced close to the man's neck, severing his leather necklace. A thin line of blood appeared near his throat. Keyes hissed with rage and flew at him. Tom side-stepped and brought his sword down in a classic counter-stroke that would have lopped off his opponent's arm.

Would have.

A second before his sword could meet its target, Tom was shoved violently in the back. He toppled off the box, landing in a painful heap on the floor. Before he could get up again, Keyes thrust his sword towards his chest. Tom looked up into the man's murderous red eyes. Cowering in Keyes' shadow was his smaller companion, Wright. It must have been he who had crept up behind Tom and pushed him over.

Keyes laughed throatily, exposing his evil, wolf-like teeth. 'Any last words, spy, before I end your miserable existence? Care to tell us who sent y–'

He didn't finish the question, for at that moment something swung out of the darkness and struck him forcefully on the skull. Keyes' whole body shuddered. His eyeballs rolled up inside his head, and he collapsed.

Having witnessed his accomplice so shockingly and mysteriously felled, the terrified Mr Wright immediately fled. If he'd stayed a little longer, he would have seen Keyes' assailant emerging from the shadows wielding a heavy club. It may have surprised him to discover that the attacker was a girl, though she dressed as a boy.

'That was good timing,' sighed Tom.

Alice Fletcher was Tom's friend and fellow spy. She was also a prentice with the King's Men. And because girls couldn't be players, she dressed as a boy and called herself Adam. Tom was one of the few who knew her secret.

Alice kicked Keyes to make sure he was completely unconscious. 'The Beagle told me to meet you here,' she said. 'I'd have arrived earlier, only I was caught up in rehearsals for *Measure for Measure* – Will's latest play.'

Tom laughed, as much out of relief as anything else. 'There cannot be many,' he chuckled, 'who could say they had to leave rehearsals at the Globe in order to get to a warehouse at the Port of London in time to knock out a smuggler of illegal wines.'

'Forsooth,' smiled Alice, 'I do lead a strange life!'

The crack of a whip and whinny of a horse made them turn. Wright had reached the driving seat of his cart and was now spurring the horse with all urgency out of the warehouse. He was almost through the doors when an arrow came whistling out of the far corner and embedded itself with a dull *thwock* in one of the barrels on the back of the cart.

At that moment, Richard Fletcher, Alice's brother, surfaced from a hiding place behind some packing cases, his bowstring still quivering from the arrow he'd just fired.

'You're here too!' cried Tom in surprise. Like Alice, Richard was a player at the Globe and sometime spy for Lord Cecil.

Tom turned back to the cart in time to watch it disappear through the doors. He had expected to see wine spraying from the pierced barrel. Instead, to his astonishment, black powder was cascading from the crack.

The three young spies raced to the entrance of the warehouse. The cart was already some distance away, bumping and skidding along the cobbles of Billingsgate Wharf, dodging dockers, cranes and mounds of cargo. It was too far away for them to catch on foot.

'Cecil thought you two might need some help,' said Richard. 'Alas, I wish I could have arrived here sooner. We might have stopped that cart from leaving.'

Tom stooped to pick up some of the powder that had fallen from the barrel. There was, on closer inspection, a silvery quality to the black grains.

'What is it, do you think?' asked Richard.

'I don't know,' said Tom, 'but I know a man who will.'

'Sir Francis?' guessed Alice.

Tom nodded. 'My master is England's finest alchemist. He will be able to identify it.'

'Last week you claimed he was England's finest philosopher,' said Richard.

'And so he is!'

'And England's finest code-breaker, so you once swore,' smirked Alice.

'I know of none better,' said Tom, pocketing some of the powder. 'I shall show this to him later.'

'What's that in your hand, sister?' Richard asked Alice.

She held up a broken necklace. 'I found it on the floor near that man I clouted,' she said.

'I parted it from his neck while we were fighting,' recalled Tom.

'It has a strange symbol on it, see?' Alice showed the other two a small bronze disc dangling from the snapped leather cord. Peering more closely, Tom saw inscribed on the disc the letters 'I H S' within a representation of the sun. Above the 'H' were three nails. Below the 'H' was an upside-down crucifix. The tip of the crucifix's vertical line bisected the horizontal line of the 'H', forming another cross.

'What do you think it means?' wondered Richard.

Alice shrugged. 'Why don't you show it to your master, Tom. Is he not England's finest symbologist?'

Tom glared at her, and Alice smiled back sweetly. In the distance, a church bell clanged twice.

'God-a-mercy!' cried Richard. 'It's two o'clock already. We are due on stage in an hour. We must get to the Globe.'

'I will go with you,' said Tom. 'Sir Francis is planning to see the play this afternoon, and he wishes me to accompany him.'

'Ah yes, England's finest playhouse critic,' chuckled Alice. Tom aimed a playful punch at her, and she ducked. Then the three of them hurried towards London Bridge, where they could cross to Southwark and the Globe.

Chapter 2

The Popish Playwright

THE GLOBE, 30TH OCTOBER 1605

Alice did not much care for Isabella, the character she was playing in *Measure for Measure*. She was much too virtuous for her liking. When the play begins, Isabella wants to be a nun. Then she discovers that her brother Claudio has been sentenced to death for making his lover pregnant. So she goes to Angelo, the temporary ruler of Venice, to plead for Claudio's life.

Being so virtuous, Isabella accepts that her brother ought to be punished for his sinful behaviour, just not executed. Angelo tells Isabella that he will spare her brother's life, but only if she will sleep with him. Isabella refuses. In other words, her chastity is more important to her than her brother's life!

Alice found this attitude difficult to understand, and it was quite hard for her to stand up there on stage and say the words: *Then, Isabel, live chaste, and, brother, die: More than our brother is our chastity.* It was especially hard when the part of the brother, Claudio, was being played by Richard!

Alice suspected this was malicious casting by Gus Philips, the unofficial leader of the King's Men. Gus was the only one in the company, apart from Richard, who knew that Alice was a girl, and he seemed to take pleasure in finding ways to discomfort her. To make matters worse, Gus had cast himself as the despicable Angelo. No doubt this was his way of subtly reminding her that he had the power to ruin her life.

After she first read her *role* (the part of the script containing her lines), Alice went straight up to Will Shakespeare, who she considered a friend, and told him what she thought: 'I hate Isabella. She's utterly cold and heartless.'

'She is as she is,' was all Will would say, which didn't help her one bit!

Luckily, Will resolved matters in the play so that Claudio was saved without Isabella having to surrender her precious chastity. The real Duke of Venice returns and, through various complex schemes, exposes Angelo's villainy. In a final twist, the Duke proposes to Isabella. Will didn't give Isabella any lines after that, so Alice was unsure how her character was supposed to react. Would she agree to marry the Duke, or was she still determined to be a nun?

'What does she want, Mr Shakespeare?' Alice demanded.

'You tell me,' he replied, maddeningly throwing the question back at her.

'I want her to refuse him. If she doesn't, then she's even more contemptible than I thought. It would mean that this chastity she was prepared to let her brother die for, she now gives away to the second man who asks for it!'

Will laughed at this, but refrained from voicing an opinion. He was very good, Alice noticed, at reflecting the world, but rarely interested in casting judgement upon it. His silence on the matter did, at least, give her the freedom to make her own decision about how her character should react. And so it was that throughout the scene in which the Duke proposes to her, Alice maintained Isabella's 'ice maiden' stare.

'I'm glad you didn't accept the Duke's hand in marriage,' Tom said to her after the play. They were in the Tiring-House, a back-stage room at the Globe, where a select group of nobles (and their personal servants) had been invited to meet the players.

'So am I,' nodded Alice. 'It would have been

completely wrong for her character.'

'It's not that,' said Tom.

'What then?'

He blushed, and Alice laughed teasingly. 'Is it that you prefer my characters to remain pure and innocent…? Or dead, like Ophelia?'

'Maybe,' he smiled. 'These women you play, I like them. And I like watching you play them. But they have their lives and, it seems, while I'm watching you, that their lives are your life, and their feelings are your feelings. And I think these characters are taking you quite a long way from *us* – you and me. Our friendship, I mean. So I was glad when you – that is, when Isabella – turned down the Duke...'

'If she did, it was only so she could go off and be a nun – not to spend time with her best friend.'

Tom didn't meet her eyes. He stared instead at his feet, perhaps embarrassed at revealing too much of his feelings.

'You should remember that none of the characters are me,' Alice said. 'I know that still confuses you, Tom. Ever since you developed a passion for Ophelia five years ago, you've found it hard to separate me from the parts I play.'

She couldn't blame him for this. It had to be strange being friends with a girl who dressed as a boy and who the world knew as Adam, and then seeing her dressed as a woman on the stage. It was bewildering enough for her, though at least she knew, at her core, who she was. She hadn't given sufficient thought to what it must be like for her dearest friend. With Richard, it was much easier, as their fraternal bond long pre-dated this cross-dressing phase of her life. He knew who she was. But Tom's first sight of her was as Ophelia, and he'd never really got over it.

Alice had secretly suspected that once Tom discovered that she was a girl, his ardour for Ophelia might transfer to her. It didn't happen or, if it did, Tom never admitted to it. She recalled one moment though, two and a half years ago, shortly after a kiss they'd shared behind the Anchor Tavern, when it seemed that Tom had developed romantic feelings for her. This had stirred something in her, and she started to believe she might even be falling in love. But later, when she challenged him about it, he denied feeling anything for her beyond friendship. So she ruthlessly squashed the emotions that had been budding inside her. This had been both difficult and painful at the time, but now she was reconciled to the fact that Tom was a friend and nothing more – and, considering the busy and dangerous lives they led, perhaps that was for the best.

A breeze blew in through the open door just then, and the Tiring-House became noticeably chillier. Tom and Alice looked around and saw that Lord Robert Cecil had entered, preceded by six armed attendants. Though no taller than a boy, the chief minister certainly had 'presence'. He did not require an entourage for everyone to know at once that a man of consequence had come amongst them. Perhaps it was the all-black attire, and the long face with its dark, wintry eyes and thin, unsmiling lips. Or perhaps it was the way he did not hesitate at the entrance, or offer any sort of greeting, but walked directly up to the only other important person in the room: Will Shakespeare.

'Congratulations, Mr Shakespeare!' said Cecil, loudly enough for all to hear. 'Another fine play.'

'You are too kind, your grace,' bowed Will. 'We're honoured by your attendance at the Globe.'

'Aye, well I had my reservations about coming,' said Cecil, '– after nearly getting killed the last time I came here.'

This remark – referring to a performance he attended in 1601 when he was almost knifed by an assassin – was greeted by a burst of embarrassed laughter from Gus Phillips. Clearly ashamed to be reminded of one of the darkest days in the Globe's history, Gus swiftly changed the subject: 'Sire, we are absolutely thrilled you came, and that you enjoyed our little play.'

'Indeed,' muttered Cecil, keeping his eyes on Will. 'However, I did not care for all the popery.'

The room fell very quiet.

'The… *popery*, sire?' frowned Will.

'Aye. For instance, why did the Duke have to disguise himself as a friar? And why did young Isabella pine to be a nun? These are very popish occupations,

Mr Shakespeare. It would have been more acceptable if the characters who aspired to them were villains, and not the hero and heroine of your play. It all leads me to wonder where your sympathies really lie?'

Will glared at Cecil. His face, Alice noticed, indeed every part of him, had become as still as stone. The greatest wordsmith of the age had evidently decided that silence was the most eloquent response to Cecil's insinuations, and it was left to Gus to reply on his behalf: 'Will Shakespeare was born and raised within the Church of England, sire. His loyalty to king and country is beyond question.'

Cecil's eyes slid towards Gus. 'There are many who publicly proclaim their loyalty, Mr Phillips, while secretly remaining devoted to their foreign faith. Queen Elizabeth used to say she did not wish to make windows into men's souls. Be that as it may, when the man in question is William Shakespeare, whose words are heard by thousands of playgoers every day of the week, then I believe it becomes the state's business to pry as far as possible into his soul. For if his soul is contaminated with popery, who knows what evil ideas might then be spread to the public through the medium of his characters? That is why I am here today, my friends. The Master of Revels suggested I see this play, and he was right to do so. For when you place the evidence represented here alongside other rumours I have been hearing recently about Mr Shakespeare's family, a picture begins to emerge.'

'H-His family?' stammered Gus.

'Indeed. We know, for example, that his mother is a member of the Arden clan, that notorious dynasty of papists and recusants. As for his father, he was a good friend of William Catesby, father of Robert Catesby, who two and a half years ago plotted to overthrow the king.

This was all too much for one of the players, John Heminges, who cried out: 'My lord, if you are going to damn a man on such flimsy evidence, then you might as well damn us all! How can Will or anyone be held to account for the actions of the offspring of his father's friend?'

Gus quivered in shock at Heminges' interjection. He turned to Cecil: 'Sire, please forgive my friend...'

'There's nothing to forgive,' muttered Cecil. 'He's quite right. A man cannot be judged on such evidence alone, but as I was saying earlier, it helps to build a picture. So let's take a closer look at the man himself, shall we? We must all acknowledge that Mr Shakespeare has, in one way or another, played a part in both of the major papist plots of the past four years. It was a line in his play, *King Richard II*, was it not, that acted as the prompt for the assassin to attack me on my last visit here? And during the Catesby Plot, the playwright was, himself, kidnapped by the plotters – *if* you can call it a kidnap.' Cecil smirked cynically. 'According to the testimony of one of the plotters, this was a very comfortable incarceration, during which time Mr Shakespeare willingly accepted their commission to write a play slandering King James…'

Will had by now reached the limit of his tolerance. Barging past Cecil and his entourage, he stormed out of the Tiring-House. Alice wanted very much to run after him to make sure he was alright. But she could not allow Cecil's slanders to go unchallenged. If Will wasn't going to defend himself, then she would have to: 'Sire,' she called out – for she was standing near the back of the room. 'May I remind you that Will did not arrange for his play *King Richard II* to be performed that day in 1601. And you yourself pronounced him innocent of any involvement in the attack upon yourself. As for what happened during the Catesby plot, Will cannot be blamed for his own kidnap. I was there with him in the plotters' house, and I swear he had no intention of writing the play you speak of.'

Cecil nodded coolly. 'If he is innocent, as you say, then let him prove it. I want no more plays from Shakespeare about friars and nuns. Nor do I want to hear from him about monarchs, like Richard II, who renounce their thrones. Let his next play declare with unambiguous clarity his deep and abiding loyalty to King James.'

Chapter 3

An Invitation

THE MERMAID TAVERN, 30TH OCTOBER 1605

lice, Gus Phillips and John Heminges departed the Globe soon after Lord Cecil, and went in search of Will. They found him attempting to drown his despondency with ale at the Mermaid Tavern, a favoured refuge of poets and players on Cheapside.

'Am I doomed to dwell in the shadow of that man's all-consuming suspicion?' Will muttered, staring morosely into his tankard. 'Will he never rest until he's proved me a traitor and adorned London Bridge with my severed head? Pray tell me, one of you, how I have wronged him?'

'By being popular and successful,' said John Heminges. 'It is a measure of your status that he's been moved to launch this attack upon you. If you were a minor wordsmith penning dramas that played to half-empty houses, the Beagle could have happily ignored you. But you are Shakespeare, and when your plays are performed, the world stops and listens. Now there is a power to rival a king's. Cecil knows he cannot arrest you, and nor does he wish to. What he wants, if he can, is to use your status to influence public opinion. In short, he wishes you to speak up for Protestantism, England and King James.'

Will laughed bitterly at this. 'If he did but know it, that is precisely what I'm engaged in doing. This very morning I've been putting the finishing touches to a play set in Scotland that glorifies the king's ancestor, Lord Banquo, Thane of Lochaber. A more loyal work Cecil could not have wished for. Now I'm of a mind to toss it into the fire.'

'Nay!' cried Gus. 'Don't do that! Why, such a play is exactly what we need. It will restore us to the king's favour and therefore Cecil's. What's it called?'

'*Macbeth*.'

'A wonderful title!' nodded Gus. 'Can you not call it *Banquo*?'

Will glared at him.

'Of course, *Macbeth* it is,' said Gus hastily. 'As I said, a wonderful title!'

'What's it about, Mr Shakespeare?' asked Alice.

'The perils of ambition,' answered Will. 'A general called Macbeth receives a prophecy from three witches that one day he'll be king of Scotland. Driven by ambition and urged on by his wife, he kills King Duncan and seizes the throne. But he's wracked with guilt and forced to kill others to protect himself. One of his victims is Banquo, but Banquo's son Fleance escapes and goes on to found the Stuart dynasty of kings that ultimately produced our reigning monarch. Of course it all ends in tyranny, madness and death for Macbeth. Richard Burbage should have a lot of fun with the role. There's a lively part for you, too, Adam, as his wife.'

'By my troth, are you not Mr William Shakespeare?' trilled a nearby voice.

The four of them looked up to see a squat, neatly dressed man hovering next to their table. His beard was literally twitching with excitement. 'Sir, I have just been to see your new play, and…' He interrupted himself as he began to recognise Will's companions. 'Why, you were the comely Isabella, were you not, young man? And you, sir, played Angelo? And you, uh…'

'Escalus,' smiled John Heminges.

'That's right, I remember now. My, what a play! So entertaining! And so delightful, and rare these days, to see Roman Catholic characters portrayed as heroes on the stage.'

Will nodded his appreciation. 'Thank you, sir. You are not the first to mention the Catholic element, something I confess did not occur to me when I wrote it.'

'That is because for you it must come naturally to depict Catholics in such a way.' The stranger glanced around as if checking for eavesdroppers. Then he lowered his voice, and continued: 'You yourself are a devotee of the True Faith, are you not, Mr Shakespeare?' He paused for an answer, and when none was forthcoming, he added: 'Come now, don't be shy, sir. I know your mother is an Arden…'

'The religion of my mother's family has never influenced my writing,' Will declared. 'I am, sir, interested in human beings, be they of whatever faith.'

'Forsooth,' smiled the little man. 'I do not doubt it.' He offered a small bow. 'I should introduce myself. I am Francis Tresham, eldest son of Sir Thomas Tresham.'

As he bowed, something on his chest glinted in the firelight. Alice saw he had pinned a brooch to his doublet, and emblazoned upon it was a design familiar to her: the letters 'I H S', a crucifix and three nails, in exactly the same arrangement as she'd seen earlier on the necklace of the man she'd knocked out at the docks.

This set her thinking. If Tresham was a Catholic recusant, then might this be a secret recusant symbol? If so, perhaps the Beagle had been right in his suspicions that the smugglers were part of a papist plot.

'Francis Tresham…' frowned John Heminges. 'Were you not one of those involved in the Essex Rebellion?'

'Aye, sir, and I served time in prison for it. Indeed, I nearly lost my head for my part in that little fracas.

Still, I do not regret my actions. We must all of us do as our conscience guides us.'

After Tresham had returned to his table, Alice made a proposal. 'Why don't we offer a special performance of *Measure for Measure* to Francis Tresham, at his family home?'

Gus stroked his bushy beard, his eyes twinkling greedily. 'A special performance. Now there's an idea... The fellow is clearly enamoured of the play. And he must have pots of money, or how else did he manage to save his own neck after the rebellion? In fact, it's a brilliant idea, Adam – I'm surprised I didn't think of it myself.'

'Rest assured, you will think it your idea before the day is out,' muttered Will, eliciting a chuckle from Heminges.

'But wait...' Gus's ruddy face suddenly developed a greyish tinge. 'You don't suppose this might play badly with Cecil do you? I mean after the tongue-lashing he gave us this afternoon, to go and perform for a bunch of recusants?'

'Have no fears on that score,' said Heminges. 'Tresham may be a Catholic, but he comes from a good family. His father Sir Thomas is a pillar of society, a former secretary of state to Queen Elizabeth no less. The huge recusancy fines he pays each year are a valuable source of revenue for the king, and help insulate him from Cecil's wrath. If we can arrange to give the performance at Sir Thomas's Rushton Hall estate, the Beagle would be unable to object.'

Gus was already rising from his seat. 'Wait here, my friends, I shall go and speak to him this very minute.' They watched him bustle over to Tresham's table.

Once Gus was out of earshot, Heminges turned to Alice. 'Now what's this really all about, young Adam? You can't seriously want to get us entangled with that dangerous zealot, can you?'

'In faith, that's exactly what I want to do,' said Alice. She explained to them about Tresham's brooch and its resemblance to the necklace worn by the man she'd encountered at the Port of London. 'The performance will merely be a front for our real purpose there, which is to see if there's any connection between Tresham and those smugglers of black powder. Who knows, we might even uncover a plot! Whatever the case, this visit to Tresham's home will help prove to Cecil that we of the King's Men are loyal servants of the Crown.'

'This seems a trifle reckless,' remarked Will. 'If I am to win back Cecil's favour I would sooner do it with pen and ink, not the cloak and dagger of a spy. I am not cut from such a cunning cloth as you are, Adam.'

'Tush, Mr Shakespeare,' said Alice. 'Do you not recall our adventure two years ago, when you helped me locate Arbella Stuart at Bradenstoke Hall? On that evidence I contend you'd make an excellent spy.'

Gus returned just then, looking extremely pleased with himself. 'It's all arranged,' he said. 'Mr Tresham said he'd be delighted to host us for another performance of *Measure for Measure*. But not at Rushton Hall. It happens that he is about to go and visit an old friend of his at a place called Whitewebbs in Enfield. Mr Tresham assures me that this friend, a Mistress Anne Vaux, adores theatrical entertainments. He will write to confirm her acceptance tomorrow.'

Gus beamed. 'My, what brilliant ideas I have!'

Chapter 4

Black Powder

YORK HOUSE, 30TH OCTOBER 1605

After Will had stormed out of the Globe, it did not take long for the remaining members of the King's Men to make their excuses and depart. The Chief Minister's attack on their beloved playwright had dampened any appetite for aftershow revelry. Among the few who remained were Sir Francis Bacon, Tom and Richard.

Cecil, supremely indifferent to any upset he may have caused to England's leading acting troupe, calmly turned to Tom and Richard and asked for their report on their spy mission to the Port of London. In the course of their account, Tom showed Cecil and Sir Francis the sample he'd collected of the powder that had leaked from the barrel.

Intrigued, Sir Francis carefully deposited the sample in a silk handkerchief. 'Methinks I can guess what this is,' he said, 'but before I tell you, I must perform a simple test.' He instructed Cecil, Tom and Richard to meet him in the garden of York House, his riverside residence, at seven o'clock, where he would deliver his verdict.

Tom and Richard returned to the house with Sir Francis, whereupon the philosopher disappeared into his subterranean laboratory to carry out his test. Meanwhile, the young men found ways to occupy themselves – Tom with household duties, and Richard by studying for his role as Casca in a forthcoming revival of Will's play, *Julius Caesar*.

At the appointed hour, Lord Cecil's barge pulled into the jetty of York House, where he was met by Sir Francis, Tom and Richard. Sir Francis led them up through the watergate and along a ruler-straight pathway lined with identical, dome-shaped evergreen shrubs in perfectly square beds. It was a garden for a mathematician rather than a nature lover – although Sir Francis happened to be both.

They arrived at a large, stone-flagged, ballustraded terrace. Here, Sir Francis stopped, took out his handkerchief and carefully opened it. Taking a pinch of the silvery black powder, he gently rubbed it between thumb and forefinger, letting the grains tumble back into the handkerchief.

'It's a very high-grade form of gunpowder,' he said.

The other three stared at him in worried silence. From somewhere nearby, a nightingale warbled.

'Are you quite sure, Francis?' asked Cecil.

'Unquestionably,' said Sir Francis, his eyes glittering in the fading light like chips of anthracite.

Gunpowder...

Tom shuddered in the cool, lilac-scented breeze that seemed to carry within it faint traces of sulphur, as if a storm was brewing.

Why had the smugglers been transporting gunpowder?

These were questions that lingered in the air unvoiced, unanswerable.

'I'll need proof,' said Cecil.

'Naturally,' said Sir Francis. 'Tom, fetch me a taper.'

'Aye, sir,' said Tom. He hastened across the terrace, through the vegetable garden and into the servant's quarters of the house. After obtaining a taper and lighting it in the kitchen hearth, he carried it back outside, cupping his hand around the flame to shield it from the breeze.

'Stand back, gentlemen,' said Sir Francis as he emptied the handkerchief's contents onto a flagstone and piled it up in a neat mound.

Cecil and Richard took several large backward steps. Taking the taper from Tom, Sir Francis leaned forwards and touched it to the powder. A searingly bright flame – white in the middle, yellow at its rim – suddenly flared, overwhelming their minds and senses with its ferocity. For less than a second it burned, and then, its fuel exhausted, vanished.

'Sulphur, charcoal and saltpetre, mixed in just the right proportions,' said Sir Francis. 'The Chinese, so I've read, invented it by accident while trying to create a potion for immortality. Instead, they created the very opposite – a recipe for death and destruction on a scale our ancestors could not have dreamt of…'

'How many barrels did they load on the back of that cart?' asked Cecil.

'Eight,' said Richard.

Cecil frowned at the black stain on the flagstone. 'I wonder what their purpose can be. Do they plan to sell it – or use it for an armed uprising? If the latter, then they must have a stash of weapons somewhere.'

'What I fail to understand,' said Richard, 'is why they bothered to bring it all the way over from France. Every soldier in this country has a supply of gunpowder, and I'd wager many of them would be willing to sell it on for the right price.'

'Yes, and those soldiers have mouths, too, that talk,' said Cecil. 'If the papists are planning something, they'll want to involve as few people as possible.'

'Besides, the soldiers wouldn't have gunpowder of this quality,' said Sir Francis. 'You saw that flame – this stuff is exceptional. I'm guessing they used charcoal from alder or willow, not the charred straw used to make soldiers' powder. And the saltpetre must have been refined by some method. I've heard the French mix it with ashes, then add a solution containing alum, blood and turnip slices...'

Cecil nodded. 'Clever fellows, those Frenchies.' He turned to Tom. 'Where did you say the barrels were being taken?'

'To a Mr Roberts of Lambeth,' said Tom.

'I want you to find this Mr Roberts and discover, as discreetly as you can, why he is taking delivery of gunpowder.'

'Aye, my Lord.'

Tom looked to his master, who nodded his approval. 'You may go, Tom,' he said. 'But before you do, take this.'

To Tom's surprise, Sir Francis unhitched his belt and handed it to him.

'But sir,' stammered Tom, 'why do you give me your belt?'

Sir Francis indicated a small sheath hidden in the belt's inner lining, and from this he drew out an exquisitely crafted miniature knife. 'When you are entering the territory of dangerous men, I always find it expedient to carry a concealed weapon.'

Tom accepted the gift with a grateful bow.

'Is there anything *I* can do, sire?' Richard asked Cecil.

The chief minister rubbed his long chin. 'If there *is* a papist rebellion brewing, that wily old fox Lord

Monteagle is bound to be involved. He knows Tom and Adam by sight, but he doesn't know you, Richard. I'd like you to go to his house in Hoxton and keep an eye on his movements for me. See where he goes and who he's meeting. Then report back.'

Act Two

Chapter 5

Whitewebbs

ENFIELD, 31ST OCTOBER 1605

Whitewebbs, the residence of Mistress Anne Vaux, was almost invisible to anyone passing by along the Barnet Road. Situated near the edge of the Royal Hunting Forest of Enfield Chase, the low, sprawling, half-timbered house was thickly shrouded by trees. As a result, the King's Men, in their three-wagon convoy, very nearly missed it.

'A perfect hideaway for recusant priests,' suggested John Heminges as they rolled up the narrow, dog-leg driveway to the front door.

'It's probably full of trapdoors and secret passageways,' said Alice, remembering how she and Tom had once discovered a priest hole at Essex House.

'Heaven help us,' groaned Gus. 'We're entering a pit of papists, a hotbed of heretics.'

'Then, if Lord Cecil is to be believed, I should feel right at home,' remarked Will Shakespeare.

They were greeted at the front door by Francis Tresham.

'Welcome, my friends. A pleasant journey, I trust? You made good time. It's only just past midday. Mistress Anne sends her apologies. She is currently tied up with household matters, but will join us as soon as she can... Ah, here is the groom to see to your wagons and horses. As for you, gentlemen, come with me and I shall offer you some sustenance.'

After luncheon, the King's Men began to prepare for their special presentation of *Measure for Measure*, scheduled for that evening. They set up the stage and scenery in the Great Hall, and it did not take long for the atmosphere in this tranquil chamber to start to resemble the chaos of the Tiring House during the build-up to a performance.

While Alice was adjusting her 'Isabella' wig, she could hear floating down from the stage behind her the mellow baritone of Richard Burbage as he rehearsed the part of the Duke. Rising above this were the screechy tones of Henry Condell haranguing poor

Timothy, the props man, because the feather in his hat was 'far too small for the character of Lucio'. And out of the corner of her eye, she could see Robert Armin, a player with an artistic bent, retouching the wooden, decapitated head of the executed prisoner needed in Act IV Scene iii. Meanwhile, Gus Phillips was going around offering help and advice to everyone, and generally getting in the way.

Home sweet home! thought Alice.

At some stage during all this, a hush descended upon the hall. Alice turned in her chair to see who had arrived. Standing in the entrance was a short, plainly attired woman in her early forties. From her erect, confident stance, Alice instinctively guessed this to be the owner of Whitewebbs. The lady had a small, firm mouth, a strong nose and grey eyes that seemed kindly yet also earnest. The eyes of a nun, Alice decided. And the crucifix worn prominently on her chest further advertised her piety. There was something faintly familiar about her, and Alice wondered if she'd encountered her portrait in one of the grand houses they'd visited on their tours.

'Welcome, King's Men,' she said in a low voice that effortlessly carried to every corner of the room. 'I am Anne Vaux. I trust you have everything you need.'

'Greetings, Mistress,' answered Gus with a small bow. 'We are well looked after. Thank you for granting us the honour of performing for your household this evening.'

'The pleasure will be all ours I'm sure,' she said, before turning to go.

Alice rose from her seat and followed the lady out of the hall. She wasn't quite sure why, but she was intrigued by her and wished to get to know her better. She entered a corridor in time to see Anne about to disappear through a doorway. The sweet, elegant pluckings of a lute flowed from the room.

'Mistress?' called Alice.

Anne turned, and smiled. 'Yes, my dear. How can I help you?'

'May I speak with you a moment?'

'Of course. Come into the withdrawing room.'

The withdrawing room was, Alice decided, a much friendlier place than the gloomy great hall. It had colourful rugs, chairs with cushioned seats, warm-toned oak panelling and a large window with stained glass. In one corner, near a virginal, a man in priest's vestments sat playing the lute. His grey hair and beard suggested he was several years older than Mistress Anne. Yet there was a strength and vitality to his features that made him seem almost ageless. His fingers moved with practised dexterity along the fretboard, and the music he produced was extraordinarily beautiful.

'What is your name, young lady?' Anne asked.

'I am Adam,' said Alice, removing her wig to reveal her cropped hair.

'Pray forgive me,' said Anne, blushing slightly. 'I thought–'

'Truly, it is nothing. A common mistake. I am performing the part of a lady in this evening's entertainment.'

The priest stopped playing. His eyes, which had been closed in concentration, now opened, and twinkled at the sight of Anne.

'This is Father Henry Garnet, a Jesuit priest,' she said. 'Henry, this is Adam, one of the players who will be performing tonight.'

Henry nodded a welcome.

Alice couldn't help noticing an easy affection in the looks that passed between the priest and Anne. They reminded her of a long-married couple.

As the priest resumed his playing, Anne invited Alice to come and sit next to her on a settle near the hearth.

'What did you wish to speak to me about, Adam?' she asked.

Alice wasn't at all sure what she wished to speak to Anne about – only that she wanted to know more about her. She glanced around the room, hoping for some inspiration. A painting on a nearby wall depicted two young children, a boy and girl, dressed up in fine clothes with lace ruffs. Next to the painting was a cabinet, its shelves filled with toys – dolls, a spinning top, wooden skittles and a miniature rocking horse.

Alice wondered why a middle-aged spinster would keep a collection of children's toys? Were they keepsakes from her youth? Or playthings to take out during visits from a niece and nephew – the children in the painting, perhaps? Neither of these theories seemed quite right though, for the toys were all in perfect condition and looked as if they had never been played with.

It was a mystery that made the lady even more fascinating to Alice – yet she decided not to ask her about it, worried that it might be perceived as too intrusive.

Instead, she opened with a question on a subject of even greater fascination to her. 'You are Catholic, are you not, Mistress?'

'Aye,' said Anne.

'Forgive me for asking, but is it difficult, practising your faith in a Protestant country?'

'Truly!' sighed Anne, seemingly happy to unburden herself. 'Each day is a struggle. But I take inspiration from the early Christians, who faced far worse persecution at the hands of the Romans, yet never wavered in their faith. They placed their trust in God, and in time God converted the Romans to Christianity. In the same way, God will one day bring England back to the true faith. That is my belief, and Father Henry's also.'

'What do you think of Catholics who aren't prepared to wait for that day? I mean those who wish to restore Catholicism by force.'

'They are wrong,' said Anne simply. 'And by their actions, they taint us all.'

Alice was comforted by these words. Still, she wondered if the lady knew about the violent past of her guest, Francis Tresham. This thought reminded her of the strange symbol she'd seen on Tresham's brooch, and its similarity to the one on the smuggler's necklace. Perhaps Anne, being Catholic, could tell her what it meant.

'Mistress, I wonder if you have some paper and a quill to hand. I would like to draw something for you – an emblem I have seen recently. You may be able to interpret it for me.'

'Is it a Catholic emblem?' asked Anne.

Alice nodded.

'Then maybe I can.'

Anne summoned a servant who, in reasonable time, furnished them with writing materials and a small table.

Alice drew the symbol as best she could from memory.

'Why, it's a Christogram,' said Anne at once. 'The letters IHS are the first three letters of *Jesus* in Greek: iota, eta, sigma. You see, *Jesus* is written out like this…'

She wrote the letters down beneath Alice's drawing:

$$\mathrm{I\,H\,\Sigma\,O\,Y\,\Sigma}$$

'As for the sun symbol, the nails and the crucifix, they are the special symbol of the Jesuits. Yet there is something wrong with the image…' She turned to the priest. 'Henry!'

Father Henry stopped playing and looked up.

'Come over here please,' beckoned Anne. 'We have a puzzle for you.'

The priest put down his lute and came over.

'Adam drew this,' explained Anne. 'It's a version of the Jesuit Christogram he's seen recently.'

Henry studied the symbol, his expression turning grim. 'Where did you see this?' he demanded of Alice.

Alice hesitated. She hadn't anticipated such a fierce reaction. Should she be treading more carefully? Tresham was, after all, their guest.

'Tell me, I pray you,' said Henry, more gently this time.

'It was on a brooch worn by Mr Francis Tresham,' Alice told him.

'Is that so,' he growled. 'Well Tresham'll know better than to wear it in front of *me*. He knows I'd kick him out of this house if he did.'

'You would?' cried Anne. 'Why? Does it offend you?'

'Greatly,' said Henry. 'And it should offend you, too, Anne. It may resemble the holy Jesuit symbol, yet it represents a malign and twisted version of our faith. See how in this version the nails are placed at the top instead of where they should be, at the bottom. And the crucifix, which dangles upside down from the H over here, should be at the top, and the right way around. Alas, they've harnessed the power of our symbol for their own evil ends.'

'They?' asked Alice.

'I mean the Catholic society who use it as their insignia – a society so secret, they do not even have a name. They are fanatics, dedicated to the violent overthrow of the king of England and his government.'

'And Francis Tresham has joined them?' said Anne, frowning. 'This I find hard to believe. And yet, perhaps not, coming as it does on top of other news…'

'What news, my dear?' asked Henry.

Anne opened her mouth to speak, then paused as if unsure whether to do so. She turned to Alice. 'You seem a kind and honourable young man, Adam. I beseech you to keep what I have to say in the strictest confidence.'

'Of course,' said Alice somewhat breathlessly.

Anne placed her hands together on her lap. 'You may not know this, but I have lived most of my adult life in the recusant world,' she said. 'I know everyone, and they know me. For the most part, we are a peaceful community. We hold our masses in private. We pay our fines, and we disturb no one. Yet lately, the mood has changed. Many of the men especially have become guarded in their talk, and less willing to share their thoughts with me. Some of my female friends and relatives have told me that fast horses are being collected in their stables, as if plans are afoot for an escape, or a gathering of forces, and this can only mean one thing… a plot is being hatched.'

'Good morrow,' called a voice from the far side of the room.

They all looked up. Will was standing in the doorway – he looked as though he'd been there for a while.

Alice was surprised to see him. Soon after their arrival, Will had exiled himself to his room to, as he explained, 'finish work on his new play'. She therefore assumed they were unlikely to see him again until suppertime.

'Forgive me,' said Will. 'I was passing along the corridor when I heard your voices. This talk of secret societies and plots concerns me greatly... In light of this, I would like to propose a change to our evening's programme.'

'Pray what do you have in mind, Mr Shakespeare?' asked Anne.

'We'll perform another of my plays, *Julius Caesar*. You never know, it may just persuade your hot-headed guest to think again about the course of action he is embarked upon.'

Alice groaned inwardly. She'd put so much time and effort into her role as Isabella and had been looking forward to giving her one more run-out. Now, on a whim, Will was cancelling the show, replacing it with *Julius Caesar*, which wasn't exactly renowned for its female parts.

'Julius Caesar,' muttered Henry. 'That's about the assassination of an arrogant dictator, is it not? Are you hoping to *encourage* him?!'

'Indeed not, Father,' said Will. 'The play is about the folly of idealism. The leader of the conspiracy, Brutus, acts from the noblest of motives. He kills Caesar in order to save Rome and restore the Republic. Yet by murdering the dictator he unleashes forces he cannot control. He misjudges the reaction of the crowd and gravely underestimates his opponent, Mark Antony. The assassination leads to civil war and a tragic end for the conspirators. My hope is that Francis Tresham will see the parallel with his own situation and be reminded that acts of violence always have consequences. At the very least, our performance will subtly alert him to the fact that you are aware of his plotting, and disapprove of it.'

'A warning to Tresham,' mused Henry. 'Well, I suppose it's worth a try. What say you, Anne?'

'I am for it, though not hopeful,' she replied. 'I don't doubt the power of your writing, Mr Shakespeare, only the ability of my friend to pay heed to the blunders made by Brutus, which is why he's most likely doomed to repeat them.'

Chapter 6

The Man at Mr Roberts' House

LAMBETH, 31ST OCTOBER 1605

*here's always fog in Lambeth…* Thus spoke Mr Keyes. And sure enough, when Tom arrived there by boat the following morning, pale rags of mist, yellow in the timid sun, shrouded much of the landscape. He stood upon a raised earthen road that bounded the river, and surveyed the scene. Here and there through the haze he glimpsed the hunched forms of windmills. To the south lay the graceful towers of Lambeth Palace, official residence of the Archbishop of Canterbury. The rest was dreary

marshland interspersed with trees and the odd cluster of dwellings.

Tom headed north along the ancient road, known as Broad Wall, following the instructions he'd been given by Robert Poley, Lord Cecil's chief intelligencer. After a short way, he came to a lane that wound west, deeper into the lonely swampland. This was Lower Marsh, where, according to Keyes, Mr Roberts dwelt. Turning into the lane, Tom passed a row of timber shacks, black with damp, perched on pilings sunk deep into the saturated earth. Looming out of the smoky air was a church, its stones as ancient and desolate with moss as the graves in its cemetery. The wet was everywhere, soaking into his shoes and through his clothes, sludgy and cold on his skin. Tom whistled a tune to keep up his spirits, and to block out the croaks of the slimy things he could hear in the bogs beneath his feet.

Beyond the church were more hovels, which seemed to float, like boats, upon the mist-veiled water. He glimpsed a face – grey and fishlike with black eyes – staring at him through a window.

Land of the wet people, he thought to himself with a shudder.

Eventually, he came to something that might actually fit the definition of a house. It was, at least, a more substantial dwelling than any he had so far seen, apart from the church. Bulky and squat, it was a single-storey construction with heavy stone walls firmly founded in the sodden earth. Stationed next to the building's side entrance was a horse and cart. With a surge of excitement, he recognised it as the one from the warehouse yesterday, now emptied of its cargo of barrels. He'd found it – Mr Roberts' house!

Cautiously, Tom approached the house. He was contemplating what his next move should be when suddenly a man emerged from the side entrance. Tom collapsed into a crouch, partially obscuring himself behind the rear wheel of the cart. The man, he observed, was Mr Wright, the diminutive companion of Mr Keyes. Wright hoisted himself into the cart's driving seat. Before he could lift the reins, however, Tom raced to the front of the cart and launched himself at him.

Wright emitted a squeal of terror as Tom seized the man and hauled him off his seat and into the road. Clamping a hand over Wright's mouth to muffle his screams, Tom dragged him to the far side of the road and down a bank into the marshes, where they could not be seen from the house. He forced Wright lower until his head was half-submerged in a shallow, stagnant pond. Wright tried to free himself, his limbs thrashing in the murky water, but his struggles were for nothing – he was no match for Tom.

'Calm yourself, I don't want to hurt you,' said Tom in a low growl. Wright stared at him, his pale brown eyes wide with fear and pleading. 'All I want from you is information,' said Tom. 'Then I'll set you free.'

Eventually, Wright ceased his splashing, and his face grew less agitated. Tom risked unstopping Wright's mouth, while maintaining a firm grip on him with his other hand. To his relief, Wright did not scream, though he still looked very frightened. 'You're that lad from yesterday,' he said breathlessly, 'the one in the warehouse.'

Tom nodded. 'Aye.'

'Why do you keep bothering me? What do you want?'

'I want to help you,' said Tom. 'But first you must tell me *everything* – who you are, what you're doing here, and who lives in that house.'

'Why should I trust you?'

Tom had his speech prepared.

'Because I'm the same as you,' he said. 'I hate the king, and I hate what he's doing to our people. I know that you are soldiers fighting for the Catholic cause, and I wish to join you.'

'You don't know me sir, or you wouldn't say such things,' said Wright. 'I may be a Catholic, but I'm no rebel. At least not until yesterday. Right now I know not what I am.'

'Explain yourself,' said Tom, puzzled by this response.

'I will do so, if you'll let me make myself more comfortable.'

Tom relaxed his grip, and the man raised himself into a seated position on the muddy bank.

'My name is Kit Wright,' he said. 'I met Mr Keyes a few weeks ago at a secret mass I attended in Eastcheap.

He told me he was seeking a carter for a small job – he wouldn't say what – and asked if I'd be willing to help. I said I might be and enquired of him exactly what I'd be transporting. He replied that it was no business of mine and I'd do better not to ask such questions. So I told him very politely in that case that I would not do it, as I never transported anything unless I knew what it was.

'I hoped he would leave me alone then, but he didn't. He kept asking me to help him, for it seemed I was the only fellow he knew of in the Eastcheap fraternity with a cart of the necessary size and sturdiness for his requirements. But since he refused to divulge what those requirements were, I continued to say no. Eventually he turned nasty. He told me he had friends, dangerous friends, who would hurt me if I did not do as he asked. So, out of fear for my life, I agreed.

'Yesterday, I went to the warehouse where we had arranged to meet. He vowed there would be no trouble, so I was surprised when you appeared, and then, when Mr Keyes was struck down by that friend of yours, I panicked and fled. Why *did* you and your friend attack Mr Keyes, young sir?'

'Mr Keyes is a very bad individual,' Tom improvised. 'He may be working for Mr Roberts, but Mr Roberts would do well not to associate himself with such a rogue. By attacking him, we were merely protecting Mr Roberts' interests – though he did not know it, and I would be grateful if you did not to mention the matter to him. Now pray continue with your story.'

Kit nodded. 'My first instinct was to toss those barrels in the river and go home, but then I thought to myself, what if Mr Keyes is still alive and he came after me? Or, if not him, then one of those dangerous friends of his. So I decided my safest course of action would be fulfil my side of the bargain and deliver the barrels to Mr Roberts, then disappear. But that's not what happened…'

'What *did* happen?' urged Tom.

'What happened was that Mr Roberts immediately hired me to work for him.'

'Could you not say *no*?'

'If you ever meet Mr Roberts, you'll discover that he is not a man who takes kindly to hearing that word.'

'Is Mr Roberts a rebel Catholic?'

'I suppose he must be,' said Kit.

'Do you know anything else about him?'

Kit shook his head.

'What is he planning to do with the barrels?'

'I know not.'

'Have you seen any weapons in the house? Matchlocks? Wheel locks? Hand cannons? Anything like that?'

'Nay.'

'And what has Mr Roberts asked you to do for him?'

'My first task was to unload the barrels and store them in a small building behind the house. This morning he instructed me to go and stable my horse and cart at an inn down the road. From there I was to take a fast horse and deliver a message to a friend of his at a place called Whitewebbs in Enfield. He drew me a map so I could find it. I was about to set off when you jumped on me.'

'Where is the message he gave you?' asked Tom.

Kit took a scroll out of his shoulder bag and handed it to Tom. The scroll was sealed. If Tom opened it, Mr Roberts was sure to find out, ruining any chance he had of infiltrating the plot.

He returned the message to Kit, and sighed. *What should he do now?* For someone so willing to talk, Kit had told him next to nothing of value. He couldn't very well go back to Cecil with such paltry intelligence. His only hope of discovering more was to try and get close to Mr Roberts himself.

'Have you told Mr Roberts what happened at the warehouse?' Tom asked.

'I didn't dare,' shuddered Kit.

'Did he not notice the arrow hole in the barrel?'

'Nay, though I dare say he will do soon enough, and then perhaps I will be forced to tell him what happened. I pray he won't be too angry.'

'Don't tell him,' said Tom, a plan now forming in his mind.

'So then what…?'

'Leave it all to me.'

'*You?*'

'Aye. He's at home now, I take it?'

Kit nodded.

'Then you must go. Stable your carthorse, and deliver the message to Whitewebbs. While you're gone, I shall introduce myself to Mr Roberts. By the time you return, the arrow hole will be explained, and I shall have persuaded Mr Roberts to employ me in your place.'

'How will you do that?' gasped Kit.

'Never mind how,' said Tom. 'Is this not what you wanted? You'll be free to go your way and never set eyes on these people again.'

Kit grasped Tom's hand in both of his, his face shining with a desperate kind of gratitude. 'I am indebted to you, lad.'

'This isn't the life for you, Kit,' said Tom. 'But for a rebel soul like mine, it's perfect. Mr Keyes recruited the wrong man.'

After a final, grateful squeeze of Tom's shoulder, Kit clambered up the bank and scurried across the road to his horse and cart. Tom watched from behind a tuft of marsh grass as the little man mounted the driver's seat, flicked his whip and trotted away.

Tom remained there for several more minutes, putting the finishing touches to his plan. Then he climbed back up to the road, brushed the mud from his coat and breeches, strode over to the house, and knocked on the door.

There was no reply. So Tom knocked again, loudly enough, he hoped, to rouse the slumbering Mr Roberts or his manservant.

Eventually, the door creaked open.

The man who answered it was tall and powerfully built. He had dark eyes and glossy, reddish-brown hair that fell to his shoulders. Tom saw that the man had been interrupted in the midst of some act of physical exertion, for he was short of breath and his tanned face gleamed with sweat.

'Can I be of service?' he huffed.

'Are you Mr Roberts?' asked Tom.

'Nay,' responded the man. 'Who wants him?'

'I am… Claudio.' Safer to use an alias, thought Tom, and this was the first name that came into his head – recalled from the play he'd seen at the Globe the day before.

As the man's breath grew calmer, his eyes became steadier, more watchful. He had large pupils, strangely empty at their centres, making Tom feel like a fly being watched by a lizard.

'And what is your business, Claudio?'

'I wish to offer Mr Roberts an apology,' said Tom.

'An apology for what?'

'It's a private matter between myself and Mr Roberts. Would you mind informing him that I am here?'

The man's shoulder muscles tensed at this, and Tom immediately knew he had miscalculated. This was not someone to be brushed aside or dismissed as a mere errand boy.

'Mr Roberts is not in the habit of speaking with strangers. But he's very interested in strangers who wish to speak with *him*.' The man drew a long, recently sharpened sword from his belt and trained it upon Tom's Adam's apple. 'I strongly advise you to tell me what you want, young Claudio.'

Tom swallowed as his eye travelled the glinting length of the blade. The sword was remarkably still, considering the man was still breathing quite heavily. He wondered who this character was? He seemed far more than a manservant. In a flash of insight, Tom realised that it had to be Mr Roberts. He was pretending to be someone else until he could be sure that Tom was to be trusted – only then would he reveal his true identity. It was therefore up to Tom to gain his trust – a tricky thing to do at sword point. He would have to choose his words very carefully.

'I'm a sailor,' Tom said. 'I was on the ship from France that delivered your gunpowder…' He stopped. The man's pupils had contracted sharply when he said the word *gunpowder*. The blade at his throat edged closer. Tom envisioned himself on the edge of a precipice. A single misstep could send him plunging to his death. Breathing deeply, he continued: 'It g-grieves me to report that while we were at sea, one of our crew became a little, uh, drunk and… well, it seems he fired an arrow into one of the barrels, which caused some of the powder to… uh, leak out.'

Again Tom paused, awaiting and dreading the man's reaction. But Mr Roberts – if it was he – said nothing. He just remained extremely still and tense, like the coiled spring Tom had once glimpsed in Sir Francis Bacon's Nuremberg clock.

'I wish to make amends for this unfortunate incident,' Tom told him, 'by offering my services to, um, Mr Roberts in any capacity he sees fit. Furthermore, I beseech you that no blame be attached to Mr Wright in this affair. When I met with him at the port, I urged him to say nothing about the damaged barrel, for it was my strong wish to explain everything to you, I mean to Mr Roberts, in person. As I was arriving here, I happened to see Mr Wright about to set off on his horse and cart. He informed me that he is currently in Mr Roberts' employ, but unhappily so. I do hope that Mr Roberts will see fit to employ me in his stead.'

'What happened to Keyes?' the man demanded, inching the blade still closer until Tom could actually feel its tip graze the skin of his neck. '*He* was supposed to be there to meet you at the port, not Wright.'

'I know of no K-Keyes,' Tom stammered.

For a long time, the man regarded Tom with cold, reptilian eyes. Then he lowered his sword and turned away. 'Follow me,' he muttered. He led Tom into the house, through a simple hallway and kitchen and then out again into a small yard where a few chickens strutted and pecked at the ground. In the centre of the yard stood a crudely made figure of a man. It was in fact *half* a man – just a torso and head made of sacking stuffed with straw. A smiling face had been drawn on the head, and there were multiple stab wounds in its chest, with straw poking out of the broken sacking. Tom deduced from this that his host had been in the midst of his sword practice when he'd arrived. The dummy stood on a pole that rotated slowly in the breeze, first one way, then the other, imbuing it with an eerie sort of life.

'You know, Claudio, I don't like liars!' said the man, and he flew at the dummy with his blade, hacking at it from different directions and sending it into a rocking, spinning blur. 'Mr Keyes is part of our circle,' he shouted as his sword flashed in the milky sunlight. 'We trust him. If Mr Keyes says he'll do something, he'll do it. And now you're telling me he never showed up at the port. Well that doesn't sound like him. That doesn't sound like him at all. I'm more inclined to believe you're a liar, sailor boy, and you know what I do to liars…'

Abruptly, the man spun away from the dummy and swept his sword in a low arc towards Tom's legs. Tom cried out and stumbled backwards in fright. As he hit the ground, he observed the sword slice cleanly through the neck of one of the chickens. He stared in horror at the decapitated bird, watching it stagger on for several more steps in a vaguely circular path before keeling over. The head, its beak open, eyes like frozen beads, lay on its side in the dust.

'I'm not a liar,' groaned Tom. 'I'm… I'm a part of your circle. I want to help you.'

'Prove it,' spat the man.

Tom opened his mouth, but he knew his tongue couldn't save him now. This man didn't want more words. So he pulled back his sleeve, exposing the fish-shaped scar on his forearm. He'd been given the scar – a secret symbol used by rebellious Catholics – by a crazed priest two and a half years earlier, during his involvement in the Catesby Plot. It had worked for him before – maybe it could do so again.

The man squinted at it for a moment, and Tom was relieved to see surprise and respect dawning in his eyes. 'Who gave you that?'

'Father William Watson,' said Tom. 'We shared a cell in the Clink when I was imprisoned for recusancy.'

The man nodded. 'Perhaps I was mistaken about you,' he muttered. 'Though I do still wonder what could have happened to our Mr Keyes. Still, I suppose this gives you credentials, doing time with the martyr Father Watson. It would be wrong of me to deny you an audience with Mr Roberts.'

Tom frowned. 'So you aren't Mr Roberts then?'

'Nay, of course not,' the man laughed as he sheathed his sword and led him back inside the house. 'My name is Guido Fawkes.'

Chapter 7

The Wild Side

HOXTON, 31ˢᵀ OCTOBER 1605

Richard had always loved the countryside and was never happier than when wandering alone through a meadow, copse or grove with nothing but birds and squirrels for company. Hoxton, to the north of the city, was not quite the countryside, but its fresh air and open fields made it a pleasant change from the packed, foul-smelling streets of London.

The day was sharp and bright with a cold breeze that cut like a knife through his thin tunic. As he strolled northwards along the Pimlico Path, Richard saw men out with their sons in the fields practising archery, and anglers huddled in their woollen cloaks hanging their rods over streams. It was a peaceful scene that belied the area's wild reputation. For Hoxton was well-known as a hangout of papists, zealots, outcasts and highwaymen, a place of raucous merry-making and violent brawls. Seven years ago, in one of these tranquil fields, the playwright Ben Jonson – a friend of Will Shakespeare's – had killed the actor Gabriel Spencer in a duel.

Hoxton existed on the edge of both the city and the law, which made it an ideal habitat for William Parker, Lord Monteagle. The wily old papist had been suspected of involvement in numerous plots against the government stretching back to the 1590s. He'd have lost his liberty, and most probably his head, years ago were it not for his usefulness to Cecil. Monteagle had deep connections with the Catholic community and had proven willing, on occasion, to share intelligence of plots with the authorities, and this had made him simply too valuable to get rid of. It was Cecil's hope that Monteagle might know something about a 'gunpowder plot' that had prompted him to send Richard to Hoxton.

The Pimlico Path led Richard past a tavern once owned by Ben Pimlico, after whom the path was named. The publican's legendary nut-brown ale had been the cause of a great deal of drunkenness and brawling down the years, including the fateful clash between Ben Jonson and Gabriel Spencer in 1598.

A little further along, Richard came to a large, moated manor house, residence of the Portuguese ambassador to England, well known for inviting local Catholics to celebrate mass in his private chapel. His property bordered another of similar size and style belonging to the famous English Catholic Sir Thomas Tresham. These days, Tresham resided in Rushton Hall, Northamptonshire, but his daughter still lived here in Hoxton, together with her husband, Lord Monteagle.

Richard had some experience of breaking into the grounds of large houses. After he and Alice ran away from the orphanage, they had endured a wretched autumn and winter on London's streets, begging and stealing to survive. And occasionally, when they were really desperate, they would sneak into townhouse gardens and help themselves to the fruit and vegetables they found growing there.

Monteagle's property was surrounded by a high brick wall. Richard began tracing a route around the wall, searching for a place where security was lightest. Disappointingly, the wall presented a uniformly smooth-surfaced, perfectly straight barrier running mainly through open cattle pasture. Not a single tree of any size could be found growing near the wall to give Richard cover as he scaled it. Moreover, the entire boundary lay within the sightline of anyone watching from the upper storey windows of the house, or from the porter's lodge near the gate. Tresham had clearly thought about security when he built the house. It would be next to impossible for anyone to sneak into the property without being observed.

Somewhat disheartened, Richard wandered back towards Ben Pimlico's tavern, where he planned to consider his options over a tankard of watered-down ale. But before he arrived there, on a grassy patch outside the tavern, he witnessed a brawl erupting. As Richard drew closer, he saw it wasn't so much a brawl as a beating. Three local men, farm labourers to judge from their dress and clearly the worse for drink, were picking on a small man in servant's livery. They had him surrounded and one was pointing a finger aggressively in the servant's face, which was sporting a fresh red bruise.

Richard slowed. His hand instinctively reached for his shoulder, only to find his bow wasn't there, and he had to remind himself that he was no longer living in the forest, and neither was it appropriate for one of the king's spies to involve himself in a public fracas. *Leave them alone*, he urged himself. *This is not your affair*. But as he began to edge around the men, one of the labourers struck the servant hard in the cheek, knocking him to the ground.

This was too much.

Ignoring the assailants, Richard strode over to their dazed victim. 'Are you alright?' he asked him, crouching by his side.

'I uh…' The man was blinking. He seemed confused.

Before Richard could help the man, a rough hand clasped his collar and he was yanked backwards. 'Keep out of it, stranger,' slurred a red-faced labourer.

Richard rose to his full height, which was several inches lower than the shortest of the labourers, and glared at them. They glared back through drink-glazed eyes.

'What's he done to deserve this?' Richard asked.

'He's a filthy papist,' said one of them.

'And a heretic,' said another.

'And a traitor,' added the third.

Richard glanced down at the man, who was moaning and rubbing his bruises.

'*You* look like a Romanist too,' one of the labourers said to Richard, pushing him in the chest and causing him to stagger.

Ignoring him, Richard helped the servant to his feet. The servant cowered before the simmering, hate-filled stares of his persecutors. Richard took hold of his arm and began leading him away. He tried to remain calm, though his heart was banging away like a drum at a country dance. One of the men came up behind him and shoved him in the back, but he continued walking.

'You didn't answer us,' the man taunted. 'Are you one of *them*? I'll bet you are. So what are you plotting this time, papist? Always plotting, aren't you, with your slimy foreign friends.' Richard could hear the labourer's wheezing breath as he kept pace with them.

'Plotting for the King of Spain to come over here with his army and take us over, are you? Plotting to make us all speak Latin and go down on our knees to the Pope. That's what you're praying for, eh?' The man cackled. He punched Richard again, hard, between the shoulder blades.

Richard whirled around. The labourer was slow to react, and Richard's fist smashed into his cheek. He keeled over. Anger blazed in the faces of his friends, who were following closely behind, and they immediately lumbered into attack.

'Run!' Richard hissed to the servant, and the two of them began sprinting away, heading north up the Pimlico Path, trailed by fuming curses and the thunder of pounding boots. The path curved west, taking them briefly out of sight of their pursuers. Richard grabbed his companion and hauled him off the road. They leapt over a muddy ditch and dived beneath the tangled, thorny branches of an overgrown bush.

'Stay down and keep quiet,' he whispered to the servant.

The labourers staggered on by, and the servant began giggling hysterically, until Richard clamped a hand over his mouth.

'I said *keep quiet*!'

In this uncomfortable posture they remained for several minutes.

Finally, the servant mumbled something, and Richard removed his hand. 'Is it safe to unearth ourselves?' the servant asked.

'Quiet!' admonished Richard, and he fastened his hand back over the servant's maw, just as the labourers returned along the road.

The servant whimpered with fright, causing the bigger of the men to lurch to a halt. 'What was that?' he grunted, peering at the bush.

Richard pressed himself deeper within the branches, keeping his palm clenched to the servant's lips. He could hear the man's quivering nostril breaths against his earlobe.

'A pied wagtail,' said the other labourer. 'That's its call.'

'What? At this time of year? You boil-brained toad! All the wagtails have flown south by now.'

'Not always. Come now, John. We're wasting time.'

'We have to find those wretches – most of all that mugwump who struck poor Henry. I'm going to tear the scullion apart with my bare hands.'

'Well you won't find them here. Come now, let me buy thee an ale.'

The men continued on their way.

After several further minutes, Richard was satisfied that the men had gone for good. He released his hold on the servant's chops, and the pair emerged from the bush and stretched their cramped limbs.

'Gramercy, my friend,' gushed the servant. 'I owe you my life.'

'It's lucky for you I arrived in time,' said Richard. 'This place is full of danger.'

'I know it, and I will take more care if I ever find myself in these parts again.'

'Why did they start on you like that?'

'I know not. I merely asked them for directions, and it provoked them to mockery, abuse and then violence.'

'Directions to where?'

'To the house of Lord Monteagle. I have a letter for him.'

This information pricked Richard's interest.

'Indeed?' he said. 'Then it is no wonder they took offence. Lord Monteagle is a notorious papist.'

The servant turned away, his bruised cheek burning redder than ever. 'As am I, sir. A papist, I mean, not notorious, for I am nothing more than a lowly groom. But a papist? Aye. Those men who beat me were right enough about that.'

'Did the men inform you where Lord Monteagle lived?'

The groom uttered a bitter laugh. 'Nay, sir. They had no time for that, for it was all taken up with calling me names and warming their fists upon my face.' Then he paused. 'Why sir, do *you* know where he lives?'

'Aye,' said Richard, 'and I can tell you if you wish, but to get there you would need to traverse a most dangerous part of Hoxton and you are, I would suggest, and not meaning to be rude, an easy target. It would be better for you to hand me the letter and I will deliver it.'

The groom appeared tempted by the idea, yet hesitant. 'The letter is of great importance,' he said.

'I was instructed to place it directly in his lordship's hands. I would like to trust you with it, yet I know nothing about you…'

Richard, having anticipated this, merely shrugged as if the matter was of little importance to him. 'I saved your life, did I not?' he said. 'I could have walked on by. But I chose to help you. Now here I am again, trying to help you. You may spurn my offer if you wish. It is of no consequence. By all means take your chances on the wild side of Hoxton. I wish you luck.'

He began walking away. The bait had been laid, and he knew that the groom would soon cry out, as he did:

'Wait!'

Richard stopped and turned, one eyebrow raised.

From his satchel the groom drew out a parchment scroll and passed it to Richard. 'Prithee, sir, be sure to place it in Lord Monteagle's hands.'

'I will.' Richard glanced at the scroll with its plain, anonymous red wax seal. The letter was his key to gaining access to Monteagle, but it was also interesting in its own right.

'Who is the sender?' he asked.

'I cannot say,' answered the groom. 'My master gave me strict instructions not to mention his name to anyone, not even to Lord Monteagle himself.'

'How mysterious!' smiled Richard.

An anonymous letter! Now his interest really was piqued. *What could it possibly contain? Some information about the plot, perhaps?* Unfortunately, he couldn't break the seal himself. That could only be done by Lord Monteagle.

'I am greatly obliged to you,' said the groom with a bow. 'I will go now.' He raised his eyes and sheepishly glanced over his shoulder. 'Though I confess, I am a little fearful of passing by that tavern again alone…'

'Fear not,' said Richard. 'I shall accompany you as far as the causeway that will take you back to Moorgate.'

'Gramercy, good sir!'

It was early evening by the time Richard returned to Lord Monteagle's house. Smoke curled from the chimneys, signalling that the master was in residence. Richard rang the bell at the main gate, summoning the porter.

'I have a letter for Lord Monteagle,' he told the man through the gate's thick iron bars.

'Pass it through then.'

'My master instructed me to hand it to him personally.'

The porter frowned. 'And who is your master?'

'I am not at liberty to say.'

The frown deepened.

'All I can tell you,' added Richard, 'is that he is a man of high status, and this letter is of the utmost importance.'

A bolt slid back and Richard was admitted. After being thoroughly searched for weapons, he was escorted along a path towards the house, a sturdy structure of pale pink bricks topped by a vast red roof. Jutting from the roof tiles were a number of dormers, arranged in two rows, with overhanging eaves that looked to Richard like the lids of watchful, suspicious eyes.

Lord and Lady Monteagle were eating supper in the great hall, attended by a maidservant, when Richard was shown in. Lady Monteagle – Elizabeth Tresham – was seated at one end of the long table, her husband at the other. She was a dignified lady with a severe, squarish face and grey, wide-spaced eyes. Richard noticed at once that she was heavily pregnant.

Could this be good news? Might he have caught the Monteagles in sentimental mood as they eagerly awaited the imminent arrival of their little bundle of joy? Surely they would be far too distracted with baby thoughts to notice Richard sneaking a look at the letter once Monteagle had opened it. Sadly, neither of them looked remotely like sentimental or easily distracted types.

Lord Monteagle, a thin man with a solemn, rather bleak countenance, put down his soup spoon and turned to Richard. 'I'm told you have an anonymous letter for me,' he intoned. 'How exciting.'

He could not have looked less excited.

'I do, sire,' said Richard, handing it to him.

Monteagle broke the seal and unfurled the letter.

'Anything of interest, dear?' enquired his wife.

He didn't reply, but continued examining the letter.

Then he put it down and returned to his soup. 'It's in code,' he said. 'I shall look at it later.'

'I trust you are not getting involved in anything

untoward, William,' said Lady Monteagle. 'Remember what we agreed.'

'Lizzy,' said Lord Monteagle soothingly, 'you know those days are far behind me. I'm a good fellow now – have been for years.'

'But you still have friends who...' She glanced at Richard, and suppressed whatever she was about to say.

'Thank you, young man,' Lord Monteagle said to Richard, 'and thank your master, whoever he may be. Jenny will see you out.'

With a final, rueful glance at the letter – unreadable from this distance – Richard began following the maid out of the hall.

Behind him came a sudden crash of shattering glass.

The maid screamed. Richard spun around. The Monteagles were on their feet, staring at the glittering shards upon the floor beneath the casement.

'Someone has got into the grounds,' said Monteagle with impressive calm. He turned to his wife. 'Go to your room, Lizzy. Jenny, escort her there will you?'

As the women were leaving, an armed guard came rushing in.

'Sire, some local farm labourers were spotted climbing the north wall,' he announced. 'It'll be the usual gang of anti-Catholic troublemakers, I don't doubt. We have a search party out looking for them now.' The guard trailed off when he saw the shattered window. He swallowed. 'For your own safety, sire, until we're certain they've all been apprehended, I would advise you and

Lady Monteagle to come with me.'

Lord Monteagle nodded, and the couple, and their maid, followed the guard out.

In the commotion, Richard had been completely forgotten.

As had the letter.

He approached the table, picked up the scroll and opened it. This was what he saw:

Add the candelabrum to the Seven Eyes of God... Subtract 4000... Multiply by the difference between the Hen and the Pelican

What nonsense was this? How could the difference between a hen and a pelican be stated as a number?

And all those numbers beneath... It eluded him how anyone, even the great Sir Francis Bacon, could ever make any sense of this. Then he caught sight of the symbol in the bottom left corner. It was the same as the one that Keyes fellow had been wearing at the dockside warehouse yesterday. A connection! Lord Cecil had been right to send him here.

Richard knew he didn't have much time – Lord Monteagle or one of his staff would soon be back. Yet it was imperative that he copied down the contents of this letter, so that Sir Francis could get to work on it. Secreting the letter within his robe, he hurried to the door and glanced out into the entrance hall. There was no one about.

Earlier, when Richard entered the house, he'd

spotted a room to the left of the main entrance with its door ajar. Inside he'd glimpsed a desk and writing implements – Monteagle's private study, he presumed. By now the sun had set, and the study, when he got there, was in darkness. Richard kindled a taper from the glowing hearth and, with shaking fingers, used this to light a candle on the desk. He found some paper and a quill, which he charged with ink, and set to work.

He wrote in haste, his body tense with foreboding. At any moment, he felt sure the door would burst open and he would be discovered. As a result, his handwriting was a crabbed and messy scrawl, only just legible. He hoped it was at least accurate.

When the work was done, he rolled up the copy and placed it in his belt, then blew out the candle. Now all he had to do was return the original to the dining table, and leave.

As he was emerging from the study, Richard's heart very nearly stopped beating. Striding towards him from the far side of the entrance hall was Lord Monteagle and a guard.

Monteagle stopped in surprise.

'You! What were you doing in my study?'

'I… uh,' Richard's mind groped around for some plausible excuse, but failed to find one.

Monteagle's brow knotted in puzzlement. 'Were you, by any chance, looking for me?'

'Aye!' cried Richard, gratefully leaping upon this

explanation. He held up the original letter. 'In all the confusion earlier, I was anxious you may have forgotten about this. I wanted to make sure you had it in your possession before I left.'

'That is most, er, considerate…'

Richard handed the letter to Monteagle. 'Did you find those trespassers sire?' he asked.

'Indeed we did,' said the lord. 'We've just been questioning them. They mentioned they saw you earlier near the tavern. You were with someone, apparently – a strong, quick-limbed fellow. An expert fighter, so they said, who knocked their companion out cold with a single blow.' Monteagle sighed. 'I wish I'd been there to see it. We need brave folk like him to stand up for us. Our community is under constant attack from these unmannerly louts, fired up by the sermons they hear in church and Mr Pimlico's evil brown ale. It's high time someone was prepared to fight back, don't you agree? If you see the fellow again, thank him for me, will you?'

'I–I will, sire,' Richard answered.

Chapter 8

The Maze

WHITEWEBBS,
31ST OCTOBER–1ST NOVEMBER 1605

As Alice predicted, Gus was not at all happy about Will Shakespeare's proposed change to the evening's entertainment. In fact, he looked ready to burst a blood vessel. 'You want to put on *Julius Caesar*?' he thundered. 'For what possible reason?'

'As a warning to our papist friends that violent revolution never works,' explained Will.

'How very public-spirited of you,' scowled Gus.

'But of course, being a poet with your head in the clouds, you never give a thought to the practical consequences of your little whims. For example, it may have escaped your attention that we're not rehearsed for *Julius Caesar*! We don't have the right costumes! We don't have the right props…'

'It's not strictly true to say we aren't rehearsed,' pointed out John Heminges. 'After all, we're booked to revive *Caesar* at the Globe next week, and we all know our lines.'

'And I'm sure we can muddle through with the costumes and props we have,' said Alice. 'It won't be perfect, but…'

'Won't be *perfect*?!' spluttered Gus. 'We'll have Roman soldiers dressed as prancing Viennese courtiers. And Caesar appearing as a duke. And his wife dressed as what? A nun? It's absurd! What will the conspirators stab Caesar with? Candlesticks?' He groaned. 'This is a disaster!'

'It's a tragedy,' said Richard Burbage.

'Aye,' said Gus. 'At least someone agrees with me.'

'No, I mean it's a *Tragedy*! And I do fancy a bit of tragedy after our recent run of comedies. I can't wait to give my Brutus an airing!'

Gus stared at him like a man betrayed. 'Et tu, Burbage?' he muttered.

Against all of Gus's expectations and dire predictions, their performance of *Julius Caesar* was a great success.

Earlier on, Anne Vaux had sent out invitations to a number of her Enfield-based friends, and that evening more than two dozen of the local gentry crowded into the great hall of Whitewebbs, eager for a chance to see the celebrated King's Men in action.

Alice knew it was going well during the opening scenes of the first act. The gasps, the laughter, the spontaneous applause were the sounds of a crowd enjoying an unexpected night out and determined to have fun. It was true that the senators' togas were actually bedsheets, and the weapons used to stab the dictator looked suspiciously like kitchen knives. As for Caesar's wife, Calphurnia (played by Alice), she was indeed dressed as a nun, which didn't make any sense. But if the audience noticed any of this, they didn't complain. After all, didn't Brutus mention a *clock* at one point – something that would have been as unfamiliar to the Romans as the doublet and hose worn by Cassius. So weren't the costumes merely reflecting the play's own rather whimsical approach to time and history? The audience seemed to think so, or perhaps they were too busy enjoying the drama to even worry about such matters.

When the players took their bows at the end of the final act, the crowd was in raptures. Alice loved their enthusiasm, and moreover she believed it was merited, for the King's Men had been brilliant tonight. Her part had been small, yet she'd done everything asked of her. As for Burbage, he'd been sublime as

Brutus – noble, naïve, conflicted, sanctimonious, and ultimately courageous as he faced his own death.

Only one member of the audience did not appear to enjoy the performance, and that was Francis Tresham, who sat stony faced throughout. His applause at the end was perfunctory. Alice wondered if he'd taken the play's message to heart, as Will had hoped. She very much doubted it. Like Mistress Anne, she sensed that this man was a fanatic, convinced of the rightness of his cause and immune to persuasion, whether by soaring poetry or reasoned argument.

After the players had vacated the stage, Mistress Anne invited them to come and join her guests for supper. Tables were carried into the hall, chairs were rearranged, and jugs of wine and platters of venison, pheasant, bread, apples, plums and cherries were served.

Alice found herself seated next to Gus, who was delightedly accepting the congratulations of members of the audience as they came up to him. 'The others wanted us to do a rerun of *Measure for Measure*,' she overheard him say, 'but I persuaded them that for this crowd it had to be *Caesar*. Sometimes you just get a feeling for these things. It's like alchemy, I can't explain it…'

Francis Tresham appeared beside them, wearing a tight-lipped smile. He leaned in close to Gus's ear and muttered: 'A surprising choice of play, Mr Philips. I was expecting *Measure for Measure*.'

'We're artistes!' beamed Gus. 'Impulsive, mercurial.

You must always be prepared for surprises.'

Tresham did not look mollified. 'All the same,' he said, 'when you book a troupe because you enjoyed a particular play, it is disappointing to say the least when they perform an entirely different one.'

Gus's smile faded. 'Are you saying you won't pay us?'

'Marry, sir, of course I will! A Tresham always keeps his word. But you won't get the full amount, because you failed to keep yours. I'll pay you half.'

'Half!' cried Gus, rising to his feet. 'Why, you rogue! We had a deal…'

'We did,' said Tresham, 'and you reneged on it. But I'll give you a chance to earn the rest of your purse and more, if you'll do something for me.'

'And what might that be?' huffed Gus.

'I want the King's Men to travel to my family estate at Rushton Hall and perform *Measure for Measure* for me there. If you do that, I'll pay you double the agreed fee.'

Gus's eyes widened. 'Double?'

'Double.'

'Then we have a deal,' said Gus, taking Tresham's hand and giving it a firm shake. 'We'll happily perform *Measure for Money*… I mean–'

'I know what you mean,' smirked Tresham.

The following morning, the King's Men began packing up their costumes and equipment in readiness to leave. Their plan was to set off for Northamptonshire after luncheon, aiming for a first-night stopover at St Albans.

While the hired men and prentices loaded up the wagons, the player-sharers relaxed in the withdrawing room. Richard Burbage and Gus Philips played cards; John Heminges and Henry Condell played chess; Will Shakespeare read; while Robert Armin listened to Father Henry Garnet play the lute. Francis Tresham had departed earlier, muttering something about going hunting. Mistress Anne was in the kitchen, supervising the preparation of luncheon.

Alice was in the stableyard, in the act of placing the severed head prop in the back of one of the wagons, when she paused. On the far side of the yard stood a girl who was quite blatantly staring at her. She was about fourteen, and dressed like a stablegirl, in breeches, white shirt and leather jerkin. Alice wondered what the girl could possibly find so fascinating. She stared back at her, and the girl promptly turned away and disappeared through a doorway in the wall.

Intrigued, Alice put down the wooden head and swiftly crossed the cobbled yard to the door. Beyond was a large, rambling garden. The stablegirl was nowhere to be seen. Alice wasn't too bothered about finding her, for now she felt drawn to explore this new, rather beautiful space. It was a bright, cold morning, and the grass, brittle under her feet, sparkled with frost. She left the lawn to wander through an oaken arbour overhung with gnarled vines and dripping leaves of amber and gold. The low sun shone through them, illuminating their threadlike veins. In the shadowy borders she saw dog violet, honeysuckle and yellowing bracken. The garden smelled of damp earth and woodsmoke. It was untended, overgrown, and had a wild sort of grandeur. Everything was fading, yet boisterous. A decaying tree had been colonised by huge plates of yellow fungus; a flock of finches darted over a dead pond; a crimson leaf pirouetted on the breeze, lost in its dance.

Alice sat down on a stone bench next to the pond. Nearby stood an ancient yew tree with purple, flaky bark and branches cloaked in grey-green feathery needles. She felt tranquil in this place, and could imagine herself living here. She was pleased that Mistress Anne had, whether deliberately or through neglect, allowed wild nature to encroach. It was preferable by far to the overly manicured knot gardens she'd come across in London. Richard would love it here, she thought – he'd always appreciated nature – and she suddenly wished he could be here now. Tom, also. She would have liked their company, as well as their advice on what to do next.

Yesterday, Father Henry Garnet had identified the symbol – the one worn by Francis Tresham and Mr Keyes – as the insignia of a secret Catholic society dedicated to the violent overthrow of the government. And Mistress Anne had said that fast horses were being gathered in the stables of many of her Catholic friends. It all pointed to a plot – a very serious and imminent plot. What Alice couldn't decide was whether to go to Lord Cecil with this information now, or accompany the King's Men to Rushton Hall and try to learn more.

A sudden noise, close by, made her look up. It sounded like a stone plopping into water. She turned towards the stagnant pond. Its black surface, previously still, was rippling. A chill breeze, flecked with rain, prickled the back of her neck. *Was the stablegirl here?*

A snap of something wet and woody made her turn. A branch of the yew tree trembled. Alice stood up.

'Good morrow?' she called.

No reply.

'Who are you? ... What do you want?'

Something rustled within the thick curtain of leaves.

Alice took a step towards it, parted one of the branches and peered in. No one there – but she spotted a broken twig lying on the carpet of brown yew needles. Someone had been hiding here.

Rounding the tree, Alice found herself at the top of a grassy slope. Then she spotted her, the girl from the stableyard, slipping and scurrying down the incline. The girl disappeared into the dark entrance of a hedge maze that lay at the bottom of the slope.

For a moment, Alice stared in bewilderment at the maze. Intricately fashioned and carefully tended, it seemed to belong to a very different sort of garden. From her vantage point at the top of the slope, she could see the complex pattern of lines and spirals cut within the dense, perfectly sculpted green hedges, leading ultimately to a circular space at its heart. She could no longer see the girl – the hedges were too high. *Why had she been spying on her?* She'd have to find her to find out.

Alice descended the slope and entered the maze. Immediately, she felt enshrouded by its chill shadow and close green walls. She crept along the gravel pathway, listening out for the echoing crunch of the girl's footsteps beneath the louder crunch of her own. At the end of the path, she turned left, then right, trying always to maintain a sense of where she was in relation to the entrance.

Left again.

Right again.

Dead end.

Turn back.

From above, the maze had seemed logical, mathematical. Down here, with all perspective gone, it quickly became a mess of endlessly meandering paths, each one looking just like the last. A footstep on the other side of the hedge, just a few feet away, brought her to a breathless halt. The girl was close. If she could only climb through the hedge, she could grab her. Perhaps the turning at the end of the path would take her to her. She scurried to the end of the hedge wall, only to encounter another empty pathway heading off in completely the wrong direction. There was no way of reaching her quarry. She might *never* find her. Why had she allowed the girl to lure her in here?

Angry at herself, Alice turned about and began retracing her steps. But of course, by now, after so many twists, turns and backtrackings, she couldn't remember the way out either. Everything seemed both familiar and strange – lines leading her in circles, circles leading nowhere but dead ends. Alice increased her pace, rushing along the paths, choosing turnings at random, hoping pure chance might take her to the way out. As each junction led her into yet more maze, she could feel her heart quickening and the first stirrings of panic.

And then, quite suddenly, one of her many haphazard turns took her somewhere new, somewhere she definitely hadn't been before: an archway cut into the convex curve of a hedge. Through this archway lay the heart of the maze: a gravel circle with two stone benches placed opposite each other, both curved to parallel the inner curve of the surrounding hedge. To her enormous surprise, on one of these benches sat Francis Tresham.

Standing next to him was the stablegirl, still staring at Alice with her cool, blank eyes.

'I was beginning to wonder when you'd get here,' said Tresham.

The carefully curled beard, the plumed hat, marked him out as a refined gentleman, yet Alice glimpsed something hard and dangerous in his smile. This was a quite different Francis Tresham to the enthusiastic fan who had come bounding up to them two days ago in the Mermaid Tavern.

Surprise quickly bubbled into anger at the way

she'd been tricked into coming here. 'What do you want?' she demanded.

'I would sooner put that question to you, Adam,' said Tresham. 'What do *you* want.' He gestured to the bench opposite. 'Please, take a seat and tell me all about it.'

Alice didn't move.

The stablegirl's hand shifted to the hilt of the dagger in her belt – subtly suggesting that this wasn't so much an invitation as a command.

Alice was briefly tempted to run, but of course she couldn't. This maze had trapped her here as securely as four thick walls of stone. There was no escaping its labyrinthine complexity.

So, with a sigh, she sat down.

'I've brought you here,' said Tresham, 'because I wanted to talk to you in private, and there's no place more so in all of Whitewebbs than here in the middle of this maze. So let's go back to basics, shall we? Who are you?'

'A player,' Alice replied.

He laughed – an unpleasant, high-pitched, nasal sound. 'No, really. I want the truth now. Who are you really, and why did you come here?'

'You invited us to put on a play.'

Tresham nodded at the stablegirl, who drew her dagger and pointed its tip at Alice. 'The truth,' he said, 'is that you invited yourselves, within a few minutes of meeting me.'

Keep breathing, Alice told herself. *You'll get through this.*

'We enjoy the work,' she said. 'You seemed well-disposed towards us. And of course we appreciate the money.'

Tresham nodded. 'Was it my money you were interested in? Or me?'

Alice frowned. 'I don't understand.'

'Then I'll be more specific,' said Tresham. 'My brooch. The one I was wearing that day in the tavern. That's what interested you, wasn't it?'

Alice let out a gasp. 'N-No, sir.'

The dagger's tip moved closer, until she could feel its coldness against her cheek.

'Don't play games with me, Adam,' said Tresham. 'I overheard your conversation with Mistress Anne and Father Henry yesterday. You drew the symbol for them, didn't you? You made Father Henry quite cross with me, in fact.'

Alice's mind was in danger of fragmenting. She had to come up with an explanation, and fast.

Tresham sighed and stretched his arms as if bored. 'Have you noticed how this garden is almost wild in places,' he remarked. 'Apart from the maze, which Mistress Anne is devoted to, much of it is slowly reverting to nature. It's become messy, unkempt – a chaos of trees and vegetation. Beautiful in its way…' He smiled at Alice, a hard, brutal grin, showing his teeth. 'An accident could befall someone in this garden,' he said. 'A young lad could disappear. And it might be weeks or even months before they find his body, whatever's left of it.'

The dagger's cold blade moved downwards, towards her heart.

All he knows about is the brooch, Alice reminded herself. *I can explain it. I can even use it to gain his trust – if I'm very careful.*

'I… was intrigued,' she said, after a pause. 'The design interested me. I knew it must be something secret. A secret Catholic group. I–I've always… wanted to join such a group. Do my bit for the cause.'

'The cause!' Tresham sniggered. 'So now you're one of us, are you? You believe in the overthrow of our Protestant king? And I'm supposed to accept that after last night, when your company performed *Julius Caesar* – a warning, if ever there was one, against exactly that kind of activity?'

'I was as surprised as anyone that Mr Shakespeare decided to put on that play,' said Alice.

'Why should I believe you? Why should I even consider welcoming you into our circle and telling you all of our secrets? How do I know you're not one of Lord Cecil's spies?'

'Lord Cecil?' said Alice as innocently as she could. 'Wh-Who, pray, is he?'

His stare pierced her, but she did not waver. 'I believe in the restoration of the True Faith,' she persisted. 'I've met Father William Watson and Robert Catesby and Sir Griffin Markham.'

Alice was pleased with the impact these names had on Tresham. The smile vanished and his cheeks flushed. He nodded at the stablegirl, who lowered her dagger.

'When did you meet them?' Tresham asked her.

'I was captured two and a half years ago, in the Forest of Arden, along with Mr Shakespeare. During the weeks I spent with Sir Griffin and Mr Catesby at Bradenstoke Hall, I gradually came to appreciate the rightness of their cause.' This was a lie, of course, yet it flowed smoothly out of her, like a true recollection, surprising Alice herself. 'Sadly, their plot was foiled. Sir Griffin was captured and later executed, and Mr Catesby escaped, badly injured – I presume he died in the forest. But their teachings had by this time burned themselves into me. I waited, and I hoped. And then, two days ago, my deepest wish was realised. At the Mermaid, I saw your brooch, and it made me dare to believe that others had taken up the cause and are fighting for it still...' She paused and let her head droop slightly. 'You were right, sir, I confess I did have a secret motive in coming here. I wish to fight for the cause, and I pray that I may be of some service to you.'

'If all this is true,' Tresham growled, 'then you should have come directly to *me*, not those spineless, milk-and-water Catholics, Anne Vaux and Henry Garnet. They made their peace with the Protestants long ago, and it'll be the Second Coming of Christ before they lift a finger against them. But if you really are one of us, Adam, then you must prove your loyalty – not with words, but with actions.'

'What would you have me do?' Alice asked nervously.

A silvery gleam entered Tresham's eye. He rubbed his teeth back and forth across his lower lip. 'No cause, however sacred, can be fuelled by faith alone,' he said at length. 'We need money, and soon, if our plans are to be paid for. And money is to be made in all sorts of ways, including from playscripts.'

'Playscripts?'

'Aye. There are many playwrights in this country, but only a few great ones, and the greatest of them all is your friend, Mr Shakespeare. I know of a company of players, rivals of yours, who are willing to pay me a hefty sum for an original work by the Bard of Avon.'

Alice began to tremble. She could guess what was coming.

Tresham continued: 'At the Mermaid, I happened to overhear Mr Shakespeare mention a new play, lately completed. *Macbeth*, I believe he called it.'

'Aye,' murmured Alice.

'I want you to steal it for me.'

Chapter 9

An Unexpected Reappearance

LAMBETH, 31ST OCTOBER 1605

uido Fawkes knocked on the door of Mr Roberts' bedchamber. 'Mr Roberts! There's someone here to see you.'

'Who is it?' responded a low, phlegm-encrusted voice from within.

'The lad calls himself Claudio. He claims he did time in the Clink with Father Watson – and he has a fish scar to prove it. Now he wishes to offer us his services.'

A pause, then: 'Send him in.'

Guido pushed open the door. A man was lying on a four-poster bed in the middle of a drab room. His servant knelt upon a faded carpet at the foot of the bed, packing a trunk with clothing.

Tom took this in with the briefest of glances before his attention settled upon the figure on the bed – Mr Roberts, presumably – and that was when he received one of the bigger shocks of his life. Warm dizziness flooded Tom's head, his vision clouded and his legs very nearly gave way. If a wall hadn't been available for him to fall against, he might well have collapsed.

He knew this 'Mr Roberts'. He'd seen him before – and had very much hoped and expected never to see him again.

Mr Roberts was Robert Catesby.

But this was not the swaggering papist warrior of two and a half years earlier – the one who had chased them through the Forest of Arden and very nearly killed them. The smooth flesh of his face was now looser, with a sallow tinge; the neat black triangle of beard had become, like the hair on his head, straggly and grey. And his right hand – after the piercing injury from Richard's arrow – was now a bronze hook. Yet there was no mistaking the long, pointed nose, the stern set of the lips, the simmering darkness of those eyes. This was Catesby alright. Against all the odds, he'd survived, just as his friend Griffin Markham had predicted he would. It must have been hell for him in that dark forest, weak and bleeding from his wound, a fugitive at the mercy of bears and wolves. Tom almost had to admire the man – until he remembered the rage and hatred, the inhumane idealism, that drove him.

As these thoughts and observations flashed through Tom's brain, a new fear gripped him – that he would be recognised. Catesby, who had propped himself up on a pillow, was examining Tom, and far too closely for comfort.

'You look familiar, young Claudio,' frowned Catesby. 'Do I know you?'

'N-N-N...'

Oh horror! He couldn't speak!

'What's that? Stop stuttering, boy!'

'N-Nay, sir. Cer-Certainly not.'

It had been dark that night in the forest. Tom, steering the carriage along the forest road, had turned to see the horse-mounted Catesby gaining on them. That had been his first and only sighting of him. Then Catesby started firing his gun and the carriage had tipped over into a ditch. Tom had been thrown from his seat and knocked unconscious. When he awoke, Richard was there, Griffin Markham was captured, Father Watson was dead, and Catesby had fled. If Catesby had looked at Tom in the intervening time, Tom didn't know about it. Perhaps he hadn't – not properly. It had been dark, and there were a lot of other matters to preoccupy him. But Tom couldn't be sure. The man's eyes were sharp and intrusive, and didn't look as if they would forget anything.

'Why did you come here, Claudio?'

Tom repeated, as calmly as he could, his earlier speech to Guido, apologising for the damaged barrel and expressing his desire, as an ardent Catholic, to offer his services to the cause. Remembering his earlier promise to Kit Wright, he ventured the possibility of replacing him as Mr Roberts' servant.

'Kit won't escape me that easily!' Catesby chortled when he heard this. 'But we could do with an extra pair of hands in the coming days, isn't that so, Guy?'

Guido looked annoyed. 'I keep telling you old man, it's Guido.'

'You were Guy before you went off to Spain!' scowled Catesby. 'Why did you change it? And what is this sudden fashion for foreign names? Claudio... Guido... We might believe in the supremacy of the Roman Church, but we're still English to our bones! You're *English*, aren't you, Claudio? So how did you fetch up with a ridiculous name like that? Did *you* go to Spain as well?'

'Nay, sir.'

'I happen to like my new name,' said Guido. 'It's elegant and refined – makes me feel like a citizen of the world.'

'As opposed to a yokel from Yorkshire,' muttered Catesby. 'Well, *Guido*, just so you know, I'll be departing tomorrow morning for Whitewebbs for a meeting with Francis Tresham. I shall leave you in charge of matters here. You know what to do. And

Claudio can help you do it.' He squinted at Tom. 'Are you sure we haven't met before, young man? Perhaps you visited Warwickshire once?'

'I have only ever lived in London, sir.'

'Except when you were in France collecting gunpowder for us,' Guido reminded him.

'Aye,' nodded Tom quickly. 'Except for then.'

Catesby's attention had switched back to the servant who was packing his trunk. 'Not that cream-and-gold doublet, you boil-brained barnacle. I'm not attending a banquet! I want the dark green one...'

Guido and Tom left Catesby to his packing, and returned to the yard. Tom skirted the decapitated body of the chicken as he followed his new master to an outhouse at the back. It was guarded by a thick oak door, which he opened with an iron key on a chain dangling from his belt. Sunlight from the doorway shone into the windowless, single-roomed building. The eight barrels, which Tom had last seen being loaded onto Kit Wright's cart at the Port of London warehouse, were stacked against the rear wall. Against another wall was a large pile of alder branches.

Tom wondered again what all the gunpowder was for. Gunpowder provided the explosive force for firing bullets out of firearms. So where were the firearms?

'Gather up some of those,' said Guido, indicating the branches.

He held open the door as Tom lugged an armful of the wood back out into the yard.

Guido nodded at an axe with its head half-buried in a log. 'Get chopping, Claudio. We need fagots, lots of 'em.'

'Fagots?'

'Bundles of sticks.' He tossed a ball of twine at Tom's feet. 'You can bind each bundle with that.'

'How is making fagots going to help the cause?' Tom asked.

Guido laughed. 'I like you, Claudio! You keep your eye on the big picture. How is making fagots going to help us with the cause of restoring Catholic rule to England? A good question! And who knows, by and by, you may learn the answer, if I decide you can be trusted with such secrets.' He began making his way back towards the house. 'Now I must go and see a man about a boat. I shall return here later to inspect your progress. Help yourself to bread and cheese in the kitchen when you get hungry.'

For the rest of the morning and the whole of the afternoon, Tom chopped wood and made fagots. Despite the growing ache in his arms and back, he didn't relent in his efforts, determined as he was to make a good impression on his new masters. By four o'clock, the ground surrounding the log was carpeted with wood chips and sawdust, and he'd stacked up a sizeable pile of neatly bound fagots against the outhouse wall.

Tom was still busy chopping when Kit Wright returned from Enfield. As he sidled into the yard,

Tom lowered his axe and smiled, pleased to see a familiar face. The nervous, wiry Kit greeted him far more coolly: 'You told me you'd persuade Mr Roberts to let me go,' he whined. 'But now he's telling me he wants both of us here.'

'I'm sorry, Kit,' responded Tom. Of course he couldn't explain that the sight of 'Mr Roberts' had so unsettled him he'd almost lost the power of speech, never mind persuasion. Instead he tried reassurance: 'I hope by my efforts to show them that you are surplus to requirements. Look at what I've achieved so far.' He proudly displayed the pile of fagots.

Kit nodded. 'Congratulations. And what purpose do *they* serve?'

'I know not. But it's all for the cause, and it is a mighty heap, do you not agree?'

'Aye, I suppose it is.' He looked at Tom curiously.

'What's wrong?' Tom asked, self-consciously wiping a bead of sweat from his cheek.

'Are you truly what you say you are, Claudio?'

'Of course. Why do you ask?'

He shrugged uneasily, and replied: 'I met a man as I was riding back along Lower Marsh. Tall he was, and extremely thin. He asked me if I knew you, and I said I did. Then he asked me to give you this.'

Kit drew a small scroll from his pocket and handed it to Tom.

Puzzled and a little worried, Tom cracked open the seal and opened the scroll. On it were scrawled these words:

The Woolpack, 11 o'clock tonight

Someone was suggesting a meeting. It had to be Lord Cecil – the tall, thin man sounded like Cecil's chief intelligencer, Robert Poley. Tom would have to sneak out of here tonight.

'Have you heard of the Woolpack?' he asked Kit.

'Aye, it's the inn down the road, where I picked up my horse this morning. Head south from here and you can't miss it. Why? Who are you meeting?'

'No one,' said Tom swiftly. Then he hastily stuffed the note into his pocket as Guido Fawkes strode into the yard. Guido beamed at the sight of Tom's progress.

'Good work, Claudio. You're proving yourself a handy addition to the team.' Noticing Kit, his smile grew wider still: 'Ah, well met, Goodman Wright! You have returned from Enfield! Oh happy day!' Guido's charm, though dazzling, could not obscure the disturbing emptiness in his eyes. 'I was half expecting you to disappear like a rat in a sewer as soon as we let you out of our sight,' he added. 'If you had, it would have been my enormous pleasure to hunt you down and impale you on my sword. Yet here you are! Now perhaps you can explain what happened to our mutual friend Mr Keyes. He was supposed to meet you at the port yesterday, was he not?'

Tom winced. *Why hadn't he thought to agree a story with Kit about Keyes beforehand?*

'Mr K-Keyes, sir...?' stammered Kit, his eyes

darting feverishly between Guido and Tom.

'Aye, Mr Keyes,' said Guido, and his smile dimmed a fraction.

Tom, out of Guido's sightline, shook his head frantically at Kit, hoping he'd understand.

'Uh, Mr Keyes…' sighed Kit, fear and confusion by now almost paralysing him. 'H-He was attacked, sir, by…'

'By who?' Tom suddenly shrieked, raising his axe and advancing on Kit, who turned white with terror. Tom thundered: 'I'll kill whoever it was harmed a hair on his noble head!'

Guido turned with a frown towards Tom. 'You told me you'd never met Keyes,' he said.

'It's true, I have not!' confessed Tom, still brimming with fake bluster. 'But any friend of yours, sir, deserves my allegiance, and I shall slay his assailant with as much ferocity as I would anyone who, er, assailed you.'

'I'm touched,' said Guido, looking a little puzzled. He returned his attention to Kit. 'So who attacked him?'

Kit eyed the trembling edge of Tom's raised axe, and swallowed. 'Some, some warehouse thieves. They… knocked him out, left him for dead.'

'I see,' said Guido. 'Well, that explains his disappearance. Though I'm surprised you didn't see fit to mention this to me earlier.'

'I beg your pardon, sir.'

Guido nodded, apparently satisfied. 'Now I must

go and speak with Mr Roberts. Goodman Wright, you can assist Tom with his fagot-making. One of you can chop, the other can bind. I want to see a stack twice that size by the end of tomorrow.'

When Guido had gone, Kit turned angrily on Tom: 'What did you think you were doing putting me on the spot like that?' he hissed. 'You told me Keyes was a bad'un, so why not tell him so. Why did you stand up for him?'

'Forgive me,' said Tom. 'I did not anticipate him asking you about Keyes. But…' – and his face broke into what he hoped was a reassuring smile – 'you did very well, Kit. You convinced Mr Fawkes that Keyes was assaulted by robbers, and now the whole problem is dealt with.'

'Until Keyes returns,' muttered Kit.

'Fie, that won't happen! He was struck so hard by my friend that even if he survived, he probably won't remember his own name.'

Tom handed Kit the axe. 'Come now, friend. You chop, I'll bind…'

The little man looked weighed down by the heavy tool, as much as by life in general. 'Why are you going to the Woolpack?' he asked morosely.

Tom measured out a length of twine. 'It's a personal matter,' he said, not meeting Kit's eyes.

That night, Tom stole from his bed in a small room behind the kitchen. He tiptoed past the slumbering Kit and went out into the bone-chilling darkness. In the yard, the swordfighter's dummy, with its manic grin, creaked back and forth, and the chickens clucked drowsily in their coop as Tom clambered over a rough stone wall and escaped Mr Roberts' house.

Raising his collar against the biting cold, Tom followed the road as it curved gently south. It was a night of moon, fog and shadows. The moon was an icy pearl that nestled in clouds and floated in copper-coloured bogwaters. The fog, like a gauzy, billowing nightgown, wafted slowly over the inky mire, obscuring and revealing, so that a dead tree turned for a moment into a tall thin man with clasping, skeletal fingers. A line of rotting wooden posts stuck up through the marsh and fog, the remains of a fence defining a long-forgotten boundary. Further on, a crooked sign, *Gurwall's Pond*, rose out of a stinking bog, and Tom wondered who Gurwall was and why he would possibly wish to lay claim to such a foul and fetid swamp. Maybe Gurwall drowned in there.

From up ahead he heard the muffled neigh of horses. An inn materialised out of the mist – the swinging, lamplit sign above its entrance carried a picture of a dray horse laden with a woolpack. He had arrived.

Tom entered the tavern. It was a rough-walled yet cosy establishment with a glowing hearth, sagging roof beams and a bar made out of old casks. Hunched over a corner table by the window were two men. Their collars were raised above their cheeks, their hat brims pulled down below their eyes, in a manner that suggested they did not wish to be recognised. One of them was so short, his feet dangled from his stool several inches clear of the floor.

With a smile, Tom approached them. 'Greetings, gentlemen!' he shouted.

They both jumped in unison, and the taller one's hat struck a roof beam, pushing it down further over his eyes.

'Thomas Cavendish,' hissed the other one, who was, of course, Lord Cecil. 'Can't you see, we are endeavouring not to draw attention to ourselves?'

'Perhaps endeavouring a little too hard, my lord,' said Tom. 'You look so mysterious, I'm surprised you haven't attracted a crowd by now.'

The taller one shrugged off his hat, and Tom was surprised and delighted to see it was his master, Sir Francis Bacon. 'There is little danger of that, methinks,' muttered Sir Francis, with a glance at the tavern's other customers, most of whom were dreary-looking men with glazed eyes and fishlike complexions.

'Why are you here?' asked Tom.

'We'd heard tales of Lambeth's thrilling night life,' said Sir Francis drily.

Lord Cecil shot him a look. 'We're here,' he said, 'for your report, Tom. Poley tells me you're now living at Mr Roberts' house as a servant.'

'Aye, that's right.'

'Good work! So what sort of fellow is he?'

'He's… Robert Catesby.'

Tom enjoyed watching Cecil's expression: it was like a slow explosion of shock, horror and delight.

'*Catesby!* So he's alive.'

'He's aged a bit, and has a hook for a hand, but aye, he's alive, and just as fanatical as ever.'

'Your instincts were correct then, Robert,' Sir Francis told Cecil. 'There's no doubting it: if Catesby's involved, this is serious.'

'He also mentioned a Francis Tresham,' added Tom. 'Catesby's leaving here tomorrow to go and meet with him at a place called Whitewebbs.'

Cecil and Sir Francis exchanged worried frowns.

'Tresham is another well-known papist, and a man of quite fanatical convictions,' said Cecil. 'If he has joined with Catesby, it does not bode well for any of us.'

'Isn't Whitewebbs the home of Anne Vaux?' wondered Sir Francis.

Cecil nodded. 'One of the more moderate voices in the recusant community, together with her friend Father Henry Garnet.'

'Let's hope they can persuade Catesby and Tresham to desist with their schemes.'

'Not a chance,' Cecil muttered glumly. 'If the good Lord himself appeared in a golden cloud and told them to stop, they'd claim it was a Protestant trick.' He swivelled his gaze back to Tom. 'Did Catesby mention anyone else?'

'Nay… But he has an associate also living in the

house – a character named Guido Fawkes.'

Cecil frowned. 'Never heard of him.'

'He used to be known as Guy. Then he went to Spain, after which he took to calling himself Guido.'

'Spain?' muttered Cecil. 'Then the plot is international. No doubt this Fawkes fellow was at King Philip's court trying to extract money or promises of military assistance.'

'That might prove difficult, now that England and Spain are at peace,' Sir Francis pointed out.

'Forsooth, the days of Spanish Armadas are gone,' agreed Cecil, 'but that doesn't mean they won't decide to support our enemies in secret.'

'Did you see any firearms at the house, Tom?' asked Sir Francis.

'None, sir. That's the strange thing. The gunpowder is there, but no means I could see of using it.'

'Unless the gunpowder itself is the weapon...' mused Sir Francis.

'What do you mean?' asked Cecil.

'Do you remember that accident two and a half years ago at the powdermill in Radcliffe, near Nottingham? It happened the day before Queen Elizabeth's funeral.'

'The explosion?' said Cecil. 'Of course! I can never recall it without a shudder. King James was in Burghley at the time, just a few miles away.'

'Thirteen people were killed, blown to pieces by gunpowder,' recalled Sir Francis. 'And you, Robert, may not have been the only one to notice the incendiary effects of that explosion, and the nearness of His Majesty. As I said, gunpowder can be a lethal weapon in its own right.'

Cecil stared at him. 'What are you saying? That Catesby and his gang are planning to blow up the king?'

Act
Three

Chapter 10

The Great Blow

YORK HOUSE, 1ST NOVEMBER 1605

he following morning, Richard arrived at York House, the residence of Sir Francis Bacon. He found the philosopher in his library reading a work by William Gilbert. Richard wasted no time in recounting his adventure in Hoxton and showing him the copy he'd made of the letter sent to Lord Monteagle.

Sir Francis's eagle eye immediately spotted the symbol in the bottom left-hand corner. 'Why, this is a Christogram, a Jesuit symbol,' he exclaimed, '– yet it appears to be upside down. How very odd. I cannot say what it signifies except that the sender of the letter is likely to be a Catholic and probably a papist.'

His attention now turned to the letter's mysterious opening paragraph, which he read several times.

'Are you sure you copied it down correctly?' he frowned.

'Aye, sir.'

Sir Francis began muttering to himself: 'Add a candelabrum to the seven eyes of God? This is beyond cryptic. In faith, it is beyond reason. What is the difference between a hen and a pelican? Well, there are many differences that I can think of, and not one of them is capable of being multiplied...' At length, he sighed and turned his attention to the long string of numbers underneath.

40~52 39~42~45~31 42~41 47~35~36~46 31~28~47~32 33~36~41~31

28~41 32~51~30~48~46~32 47~42 45~32~47~36~45~32 47~42

52~42~48~45 30~42~48~41~47~45~52 35~42~40~32 33~42~45 50~32

46~35~28~39~39 3~41~33 39~36~30~47 28

34~45~32~28~47 29~39~42~50 48~43~42~41 42~48~45

42~43~43~45~32~46~46~42~45~46

For several minutes Sir Francis said nothing, but simply stared at the digits, eyes wide, forehead furrowed, as if willing them to make sense. Then, quite abruptly, he jerked his head up and stared hard at Richard, his beard quivering.

'Have you noticed,' he said, 'that not one of these numbers is lower than 28.'

Richard moved closer and peered at the paper. 'That is true, sir.'

'And not one of them is higher than 52.'

'Also true,' acknowledged Richard. 'But where does it get us?'

'Isn't it obvious?'

Richard had to confess that it wasn't – at least not to him.

'We have a range of 25 numbers here, running from 28 to 52,' said Sir Francis. 'That suggests to me that each number represents a letter of the alphabet.'

'But there are 26 numbers in the alphabet,' pointed out Richard.

'Aye, and the last one, "z", is rarely used and most likely doesn't appear in this message.'

'So, if you're right, how do we work out which letters each number represents?'

'Simple! The lowest one, 28, must stand for A; 29 stands for B, and so on. In other words, we need to subtract 27 from each number to work out the letter's placing in the alphabet... And, oh! There's that number again!' Sir Francis's expression became distracted as his mind went on a journey.

'What number sir?' Richard prompted.

'What?' said Sir Francis, jerking back into consciousness. 'Why *this* number of course – 27 – it keeps cropping up in Catholic codes. The number 3, you see, represents the Holy Trinity, and 27 is 3 x 3 x 3, so it's especially significant. It also appears in my favourite painting, The Ambassadors, which many Catholic radicals would have encountered during the Essex Rebellion of 1601 because it hung in the house of their leader, the Earl of Essex.'

'Perhaps we ought to get back to decoding the message,' Richard gently hinted.

'Of course! Let's test out my theory, shall we? The first number on the top row is 40. If we subtract 27, we get 13. The 13th letter of the alphabet is… M, I believe.'

Sir Francis wrote down an 'M'. 'What's the next letter, Richard?'

'52.'

'Well that's obviously a Y, being the last but one letter.'

He wrote down a 'Y'.

'*My*,' Sir Francis read out. 'A promising start, wouldn't you say, my friend? It seems we may have cracked at least this part of the message.'

They continued to work their way through the numbers, with Richard calling them out, and even, after a while, doing the calculations himself, while Sir Francis wrote the decoded message down. Gradually they became quicker as Richard started recognizing the most commonly occurring numbers, like 42 (representing O), 45 (R) and 32 (E), enabling him to decipher them without the need for any calculation.

Soon enough, the message was laid bare:

My lord, on this date, find an excuse to retire to your country home, for we shall inflict a great blow upon our oppressors.

'A great blow,' Richard read. 'Could that mean…?'

'Gunpowder,' said Sir Francis, nodding his head vigorously. 'We know for sure that eight barrels of the stuff have been stored at the Lambeth residence of the notorious papist Robert Catesby.'

'Catesby?' gasped Richard. 'Is *he* still alive?'

'Evidently. This much we have learned from Tom.'

'Do you think it was Catesby who sent this warning to Lord Monteagle?'

'Possibly. Or it might just as easily have been another of the plotters. We have two more names so far – Francis Tresham and someone called Guido Fawkes.'

Richard was studying the revealed message: '*On this date* it says. On what date?'

'That is the crucial question,' agreed Sir Francis. 'Is this "great blow" set for next week, next month, or next year? To find out, we'll need to decode the first part of the message, which is quite beyond my powers.'

Sir Francis began pacing the room with quick, nervous steps. 'The question – the really big question – is this: do we move in on Catesby now, arrest him and seize the gunpowder, or do we wait until we've uncovered the whole plot and then arrest everybody at the same time before they have a chance to scatter?

My inclination is to wait and try and catch everybody. But I have to acknowledge the risk this carries, for there's always the chance that this "great blow" will happen far sooner than we expect. We'll have to see what Lord Cecil decides.'

They did not have long to wait. That afternoon, Lord Cecil's order arrived: *Make no move on Catesby yet. Proceed for now with your enquiries.*

'A wise decision,' nodded Sir Francis approvingly. 'So let's proceed.'

'How exactly?' queried Richard.

'We must pay a visit to the man who is in many ways at the centre of this entire plot – though he is most probably quite unaware of it, for he is a thoroughly honourable, decent and law-abiding fellow. Nevertheless, he may be able to help shed some light on what is going on.'

'To whom are you referring, sir?'

'I am referring to the father of Francis Tresham, and father-in-law of Lord Monteagle: my dear old friend, Sir Thomas Tresham. I'm afraid it will mean a journey, though: he lives in Northamptonshire.'

Chapter 11

To Steal or Not to Steal?

WHITEWEBBS, 1ST NOVEMBER 1605

As she made her way back through the garden, Alice tried to decide what to do. Should she steal Will's new play and give it to Tresham? If she did, she would instantly win Tresham's trust and hopefully be recruited into the plot. On the other hand, to do so would be a terrible betrayal of her friend. Will's play would end up in the hands of their rivals, who would perform it and claim it as their own.

But would that be so terrible compared to the overthrow of the king, which was the likely consequence of doing nothing? Will probably had a copy of the play, or at least an earlier draft, so it wouldn't be completely lost – yet England might be, if she didn't act.

As she was crossing the stableyard towards the house's side entrance, an idea suddenly popped into her head. Perhaps she could talk to Will about this. He might even be willing to let her 'steal' the play, once he realised what was at stake. Assuming he had a copy of the script, they could rehearse and perform it before their rivals managed to. That way England would be saved *and* the world would know Will wrote *Macbeth* – an entirely satisfactory result! With a renewed bounce in her step, Alice entered the house.

As she was approaching Will's quarters, she saw Mistress Anne coming the other way.

'Ah, there you are, Adam,' said Anne. 'We were looking for you earlier. You missed luncheon.'

'Did I? I'm sorry.'

'It is no matter. But you must be hungry my child. You should eat something before you depart with your troupe for Northamptonshire. Mr Philips has informed me you will be leaving at three o'clock. Perhaps...' She paused as an idea came to her. 'Perhaps you'd like to join me in the withdrawing room. I shall ask cook to prepare some bread, cold cuts and wassail and we can talk, while Father Henry entertains us with his lute.'

'You are too kind, mistress, although–'

'It is nothing, Adam. Go there now, and I shall be with you shortly.'

Alice was about to explain that she had to see Will about something rather urgent, but then she changed her mind; she did not wish to offend her hostess, and, it was true, she did feel rather hungry. Her conversation with Will could always wait half an hour.

In the withdrawing room, Father Henry was warming up his fingers with some scales. Alice seated herself on the settle near the hearth, as he launched into a melody. It was sad and sweet and strangely familiar – achingly so. Soon afterwards, Anne arrived. She hummed along to the melody as she took her seat, and then began to sing:

> *Alas my love you do me wrong,*
> *To cast me off discourteously*
> *And I have loved you oh so long*
> *Delighting in your company.*
>
> *Greensleeves was my delight,*
> *Greensleeves my heart of gold*
> *Greensleeves was my heart of joy*
> *And who but my lady Greensleeves.*

Anne's voice was both mellow and strong, and it beautifully complemented Father Henry's playing. Alice could not recall having heard this song before, yet she was certain she had. Closing her eyes, she let the music wash through her and carry her back to a mysterious never-time, before memory, before everything.

Too soon, a servant entered bearing a tray of food. The music stopped, and the spell was broken. The food, at least, was delicious: there were cuts of swan breast and boar leg, a loaf of marchet bread and the hot, sweet, spicy ale known as wassail. Between mouthfuls, Alice answered Anne's questions about her life as a player. She was unused to talking about herself – few, until now, had shown much interest in her personal experiences – and she spoke haltingly at first, only gradually growing in confidence. She spoke of pre-performance nerves, and the secret of a good special effect. She recalled some tricky occasions, such as the time she'd had to improvise on stage when Gus Philips forgot his speech and started spouting lines from another play, and the day Will Shakespeare, playing a ghost, got stuck under the stage because a trapdoor bolt wouldn't open. Luckily Tom Cavendish had been there to help them. The memory of that moment – the first time she ever saw Tom – made her smile. It felt good to be able to share these details with someone, especially someone like Anne, who seemed so eager to listen to and smile at her stories.

At the same time, the whole business with Tresham was still nagging at her. She almost mentioned it to Anne at one point, but then decided it might not be wise. Tresham had listened in on her earlier conversation with Anne, which was how he'd found out about her interest in his brooch. Maybe he had his ear to the keyhole right now, checking up on her.

During a lull in the conversation, Alice's eye fell once again on the painting of the little boy and girl and, next to it, the cabinet full of children's toys. She'd been too polite to ask Anne about this before, but now that she'd revealed so much about her own life, perhaps it was permissible to ask Anne about hers.

'Do you have any nephews or nieces, Mistress?'

'Nay. Why do you ask?'

'I just assumed…' Alice gestured to the cabinet.

Anne nodded sadly. 'If you look closely, my dear, you will see the toys are all in perfect condition. They've never been played with.'

Alice had noticed. 'So then why do you have them?'

'I've always loved children,' Anne said softly.

It seemed an odd, incomplete sort of answer. Alice sensed there was more that Anne could have said, but she was deliberately holding something back.

'Have you ever thought of marrying?' Alice asked.

'No,' said Anne, casting a swift glance towards Father Henry. 'I fell in love once, but it was an impossible situation…'

Just then the door opened and Will stumbled in. He looked bewildered, as if someone had just punched him in the head. 'My new play,' he said to no one in particular. 'It's gone. I think… I think it's been stolen.'

'Oh, Mr Shakespeare, are you sure?' cried Anne. 'Is it not possible that you put it aside somewhere and forgot it? I am always doing that with books.'

'Nay, ma'am,' replied Will as he slumped into a chair and clasped his face in his hands. 'The play has been on the desk in my bedchamber ever since I placed it there upon our arrival. It was there after luncheon when I returned to my room for a brief nap. When I awoke just now… it was gone.'

Alice struggled to make sense of this development. She guessed Tresham must have stolen it – or, more likely, ordered that creepy stablegirl to do so. But why? Had he decided he couldn't trust her to do the job? This was terrible news in every way. Not only had Will lost his play, Alice had no means left to her of winning Tresham's trust. If only she'd gone to see Will as she'd planned instead of allowing herself to be waylaid by Mistress Anne! But surely all was not lost – he must have another copy…

'But Mr Shakespeare, you have a copy of the play at your house in Southwark I presume – an earlier draft?'

He looked at her, and she could see in his sad, red-rimmed eyes that he did not. 'The words of my plays and poems tumble fully formed from my pen,' he told her. 'There are no earlier drafts.'

'I shall go and speak with the servants,' said Anne. 'It's possible that one of them moved it while they were cleaning your chamber. Father Henry, perhaps you could organize a search. I cannot abide the thought that we are responsible for the loss of one of Mr Shakespeare's wonderful plays.'

'Good lady, you are not responsible,' sighed Will.

'Indeed you are not,' said Father Henry, putting down his lute. 'Yet someone else is. If it has been stolen, we must find the culprit.'

Alice could no longer keep silent about what she knew. With all hope of infiltrating Tresham's plot gone, she had a duty to her friend to reveal all. But as she opened her mouth to speak, the door opened once again and Francis Tresham entered.

'Mr Shakespeare,' he said, 'I just happened to be passing…'

Of course you were, you old snoop! thought Alice to herself.

'… and I couldn't help overhearing the terrible news. Is it true? Have you really lost your new play?'

'Aye,' grimaced Will.

'I am deeply sorry to hear it. Yet I am confident that it will be found, if we all help in the search.'

'I thank you, sir.'

Tresham was almost convincing in his pretence at compassion, thought Alice. Perhaps Gus ought to invite such a play-actor to join the King's Men, assuming Lord Cecil didn't hire him first for his eavesdropping skills. She would take pleasure in pricking his bubble and exposing his villainy to the world.

'Adam,' said Tresham, casting a sharp glance towards her. 'You remember that book I was speaking to you about earlier?'

'Which book, sir?'

'The one about… um… garden mazes? I have

found a copy in the library. Come with me and I'll show you.'

Utterly confused, Alice rose from the settle. She could feel Father Henry's suspicious gaze upon them as she followed Tresham out of the room and into the library on the far side of the corridor.

Here, Tresham turned on her. The smile had vanished with the closing of the door behind them. 'So tell me then, Adam, where is it?' he said.

'Where is what sir?'

'Why, the play of course! I assume it was *you* who stole it.'

Chapter 12

The Foul Apparition

LAMBETH, 1–4TH NOVEMBER 1605

The following morning, Mr Roberts departed for Whitewebbs. And for the next three days, Tom and Kit worked for Guido Fawkes, chopping wood to make fagots and billets (big chunks of wood). When the alder branches in the outhouse were all used up, Guido sent them out in Kit's horse-and-cart to the Great North Wood, an enormous forest on the southern borders of Lambeth and Southwark, to chop down and bring back more.

Each evening they would load up Kit's cart with

the fagots and billets they'd made that day. Then Guido would climb into the driver's seat and ride off with this cargo in the direction of the river. He never told them where he was taking all this wood, but the following morning, the cart, now empty, was always back outside the house.

Kit constantly complained to Tom about the situation. 'That man has no right to keep me here,' he'd say. 'I am a freeborn Englishman – a carman and carrier with my own business and my own customers who, by the way, I have sorely neglected.'

'Then leave,' Tom would bluntly advise him.

To which Kit would snort: 'And be hunted down like a dog and impaled on that man's sword? Even if I could get back to Eastcheap, do you suppose I could go out again on a dark night without fearing that every shadow conceals Mr Fawkes and his dreadful blade?'

As for Tom, he kept focused on the task at hand, while keeping his eyes and ears open, as Sir Francis had once taught him, hoping to catch a clue as to what Guido's plans were. If he and Catesby planned to blow up the king, how did they propose doing it, where and when? Tom intended to continue masquerading as 'Claudio', the zealous young rebel, until Guido was sufficiently impressed to take him fully into his confidence.

All was going according to plan until the evening of 4 November, when something quite appalling happened. They were in the yard – Kit, Tom and

Guido – loading up Kit's cart with the day's harvest of fagots and billets. Rain had been falling from a dark sky since noon, and the yard was an expanse of grey, sticky mud and puddles. They were all dirty, and wet to their skins, and Tom was looking forward to his evening meal and bed, when he was distracted by the scrape of a nearby footstep.

He glanced up, his arms weighed down with billets, half expecting to see Catesby returned. Instead, what he saw gave him a terrible shock. Standing there in the yard entrance, like something monstrous that had emerged from the marsh, was the tall, scarecrowlike figure of Mr Keyes. He was filthy, and his clothing could no longer be distinguished beneath the mud that caked it. He stood there like a lopsided statue, oblivious to the rain that fell upon his hatless head and streamed down his face, and his eyes never left Tom.

Tom stared blankly back, as the billets tumbled from his unfeeling arms.

'Mr Keyes!' cried Guido. 'Is that really you? Or a foul apparition conjured from the mire?'

Keyes swivelled his gaze towards Guido. He raised a long, trembling finger towards Tom, and said: 'That lad should not be here, he should not be working in your employ Mr Fawkes because as sure as I am alive, he is a spy.'

Tom pressed his feet hard into the mud, trying to stop the trembling that had begun in his hands and was spreading quickly through his body.

Guido looked bemused. 'Claudio? A spy? How do you know?'

'He were at the warehouse the day the shipment arrived, watching us,' growled Keyes.

'Forsooth, he was on the ship that delivered it,' said Guido.

'Nay, Mr Fawkes. He was not on the ship. He was in the warehouse... Fought me like a trained swordsman he did, came real close to killing me, so I don't know what he said to convince you to take him in, but I swear to you it's all lies.'

Guido directed his gaze at Tom. The smile was gone now, and there was nothing to disguise or soften the blank coldness of his stare. His hand, Tom noticed, had moved to the hilt of his sword. 'Speak, Claudio,' he murmured. 'What happened in that warehouse?'

'I… I fought him, it's true.'

There was no point in denying it. Guido had known Keyes a long time, and he would know Keyes had no reason to lie about this.

Yet now he'd confessed to the fight, Tom would have to come up with a convincing reason for it. He groped around for something to say. Unfortunately, his mind at that moment resembled an empty cavern.

'Why did you fight him, Claudio?'

'Because… uh…'

Keyes leapt in: 'Because he's a spy, Mr Fawkes, as I said he's working for the government.'

Guido drew his sword and aimed it at Tom's stomach.

He seemed disturbingly calm, as if contemplating a slice of roast beef and pondering which area to cut first. 'Why did you fight him, Claudio?' he asked again.

'Because he's your enemy, sir,' said Tom.

It was all he could think of.

Keyes started to protest, but he was hushed by a gesture from Guido. 'My enemy? How so?'

'He wanted…'

Sweat began to mingle with the rain on Tom's face, stinging his eyes and making him blink: *What did he want? Where am I going with this?*

And then it came to him.

'He wanted to steal the shipment from you. He tried to force Kit to take the barrels to his house, not here.'

'*Liar!*' shrieked Keyes. 'Tell him, Mr Wright, tell Mr Fawkes what really happened…'

All eyes now turned to Kit, who seemed to crumple beneath the combined weight of their stares. Tom silently pleaded with him to back him up, but he knew there was little chance of that. Keyes' reappearance changed everything. For all the camaraderie Tom and Kit had developed over the past few days, and for all Kit's fear and hatred of Keyes, the little man's survival instinct must surely trump everything now.

'Wh-What happ…ened… What h-happened…' Kit faltered.

'We're waiting,' said Guido impatiently.

Kit tried again: 'What happened, sir, was as… as Cl-Claudio said.'

Tom couldn't believe his ears. His heart, having clenched into a tight ball, started beating again, as Kit continued in a breathless rush: 'Claudio stayed behind after his ship departed to ap-apologise for the split barrel, and he saw M-Mr Keyes try to force me to steal the barrels. So he fought him, sir. Near killed him, but now he's back.'

Keyes' complexion became as dark and grey as the sky. 'Why is you doing this Mr Wright? Why is you lying for that scoundrel? Do you want to die like a rat? Is that what you want?'

Guido's rain-bespattered sword did not move from Tom. 'Why did neither of you see fit to tell me of Keyes' betrayal?' he demanded.

'We feared you wouldn't believe us,' said Kit, 'or that you would think *us* the traitors for killing Mr Keyes. You've known him far longer than myself and Claudio. But *he's* the traitor sir.'

'Enough with your lies,' snarled Keyes. 'Mr Fawkes can see very well that your story makes no sense, for what use would I have for barrels of gunpowder?'

'Oh, I can think of a few,' said Guido, his glacial stare settling for the first time upon Keyes. 'You could sell them. High-quality French powder fetches a high price in these parts.'

'But I is your loyal partner, Mr Fawkes,' said Keyes, his shoulders twisting uncomfortably. 'I is your brother in God. We've known each other for years, and you know I would never steal from you… while *this* pair–'

'This pair have had every chance to steal those barrels these past few days, and every chance to escape, but they haven't,' said Guido. 'They've been here, rain and shine, chopping wood. I doubt you would have done so much as them, Goodman Keyes. You lack the patience for it. It's true, you and I have been acquainted a while, but I do not know you. You're a creature of the shadows. You have no wife, no children, no land. You drift. I see you at mass, but I know not what you believe. Do you believe in anything, Mr Keyes? Money perhaps. I know you will gladly take my own, and just as willingly someone else's. You have a nose for opportunities, and you'll seize them as quickly as you find them. The gunpowder was an opportunity, was it not…?'

Keyes listened in great indignation to all this, his shoulders flexing and coiling. Several times he attempted to interrupt, but he could not break into Guido's forceful delivery. Towards the end, something seemed to crack inside him. Perhaps it was a change he noticed in Guido's expression, or a twitch of the man's sword hand. Whatever it was, Keyes became rigid, his eyes like white-rimmed globes jutting from his dirty face. Then he turned and fled from Mr Roberts' house, his tall, sticklike figure quickly fading into the rain and fog.

That night, as Tom lay in bed, reliving his fortunate escape, a shadow loomed above him. He heard Guido whisper: 'Get up, Claudio, and follow me.'

A startled Tom sat up. He groped around in the dark for his clothing, wondering what Guido could possibly want at this late hour. *Had Keyes come back? Was Tom about to be killed?*

But he'd heard no menace in Guido's voice, only urgency.

Once dressed, he edged past the gently snoring Kit and went out into the freezing night. The cart was there in the yard, frost riming its struts and wheel spokes. Steam snorted from the horse's nostrils. The cart was empty of fagots and billets after Guido's usual, mysterious evening trip.

Guido's voice floated from the outhouse: 'Come help me load these barrels onto the cart.'

'The barrels, sir?' said Tom, rushing to join him.

'Aye, we're getting out of of this place, my young friend. Our work here is done.'

Tom blinked, not quite understanding. He stifled a yawn.

'I'm inviting you because I trust you, Claudio,' said Guido. 'You earned it after your exposure of the traitor Robert Keyes. From now on, you're one of us. Am I right to trust you?'

'Aye sir,' said Tom, managing to hold Guido's penetrating stare. His heart thumped loudly in his ears. *He was about to learn the truth...*

Together, they hoisted up the gunpowder-filled barrels, carried them out into the yard and heaved them, one by one, onto the back of the cart. It sagged lower and lower with each additional cask, and Tom felt some sympathy for Kit's faithful old dray horse, now peacefully munching on some weeds growing between the cobbles.

When all the barrels were loaded, Tom climbed up onto the driver's seat beside Guido, who flicked his whip. The dray horse staggered a little from the weight, then started easing them forward through the gates and onto Lower Marsh.

They headed north, towards the river. The dim lanthorn dangling from the cart threw out scarcely enough light to see more than a few yards through the fog. The road had sudden, scary bends, and Tom feared that at any moment they would plunge catastrophically into the freezing marsh. But both Guido and the horse knew this road very well by now, having travelled it back and forth these past five nights. Within half an hour, they had reached the Thames.

Here they turned south and proceeded along the river bank until they came to the little jetty where Tom himself had landed less than a week ago. A large and sturdy boat was moored there.

'That's ours,' said Guido proudly as he jumped down from the seat. 'Cost me more than a few shillings to hire it, but it'll fit the barrels and ourselves with room to spare.' He glanced swiftly up and down the empty bankside road. 'We should make haste, Claudio. I feel a little exposed out here.'

They began the task of loading the barrels into the boat, taking extra care in the dark on the slippery wooden steps that led down to the jetty. As they were conveying the eighth and final barrel down these steps, they were startled by the flash of a bright light and the creak of a footstep on the bank above them.

'What ho, gentlemen!' called a voice. 'Pray tell us what business you are about at this evil hour?'

Squinting through the light of a lantern, Tom glimpsed the ruddy face of a nightwatchman. Alongside him was another with long grey hair and beard, wielding a large stick.

Guido gestured to Tom with his eyes to continue down the steps. They were laying the barrel in the boat when Tom was startled by the crack of a stick being slammed onto stone.

'When my friend asks you a question, he expects an answer,' the bearded one barked. 'Why are you here, and what's in those barrels?'

Chapter 13

Lady Muriel

RUSHTON HALL, 3RD NOVEMBER 1605

Richard leaned out of the coach window as he and Sir Francis progressed up the long, straight driveway of Rushton Hall, home of Sir Thomas Tresham. From two hundred yards out, the house presented a magnificent façade of creamy stone, gracefully curving roofs topped by tall pinnacles, and at least a hundred windows glittering in the early afternoon sunlight.

The journey to Northamptonshire had taken them two full days, and Richard was feeling restless after spending so many hours in a cramped carriage. Now he was eager to stretch his legs, and excited to meet the great Sir Thomas Tresham, of whom Sir Francis had spoken so effusively.

'How exactly do you suppose Sir Thomas will help us in our investigations of the plot?' he asked Sir Francis. 'Might he have been the writer of that mysterious letter to his son-in-law?'

'Certainly not!' answered Sir Francis. 'If Sir Thomas ever got wind of a plot, he would go straight to Lord Cecil and tell him everything he knew. In spite of his Catholic faith, he has always been unswervingly loyal to the government.'

'Well then do you suspect he might know something about his son's recent activities?'

'I very much doubt it,' responded Sir Francis. 'The two have been estranged ever since Tresham Junior got mixed up in the Essex Rebellion five years ago. Sir Thomas had to pay a vast sum to save his son from the executioner's axe. He was so angry about that, he disinherited him.'

'So then how will he be able to help us?' asked Richard.

Sir Francis did not answer directly. Instead, he asked Richard: 'Did you remember to bring the Monteagle letter?'

'You have asked me that five times since we departed, sir,' said Richard. 'And the answer, as always, is *yes*.' For good measure, he dug the letter out of his bag and brandished it beneath Sir Francis's nose.

'Excellent,' said the philosopher. 'Now we must decode the first part of it.'

'But you told me that was beyond your powers.'

'It certainly is. But there is someone I know with even greater powers than mine.'

'Impossible, sir,' said Richard. 'Tom said you were the finest code-breaker in England.'

'*Did* he now?' beamed Sir Francis. 'Well, he may be right about that. However, this is a special kind of code involving strange Catholic terms like the Candelabrum and the Seven Eyes of God. To understand the hidden meaning of such phrases we must consult the finest *Catholic* code-breaker in England.'

'And who might that be?'

'Why, Sir Thomas Tresham, of course. That, to answer your question, is why we're here!'

They passed beneath a grand archway guarded by two giant statues of armoured knights, into a spacious courtyard. The servant who hurried out of the house to help them from their carriage wore black. Sir Francis sniffed the air as he stepped down, and frowned. 'Something is wrong,' he muttered.

On the steps leading to the entrance they were greeted by Lady Muriel Tresham, Thomas's wife. She too was dressed entirely in black apart from a stiff white ruff. A sprig of rosemary was pinned to her sleeve. As Richard bent to kiss her frail pink hand, he saw she was wearing a ring bearing a skull symbol.

From these emblems he and Sir Francis knew the

sad truth: Sir Thomas was dead.

'He passed away a week ago, after a short illness,' said Muriel once the three of them were seated in her parlour. 'I could tell he was in pain, but he didn't make a fuss. Typical of the man…' She appeared calm and composed, but her eyes were raw with grief.

'My deepest condolences, Lady Tresham,' Richard said to her.

'He was the best of men,' said Sir Francis, and he did not wipe away or seek to hide the tears streaming down his cheeks. 'I feel honoured to have known him.'

'He felt the same way about you, Francis,' said Muriel. 'As do I. You were like a son to us.'

Sir Francis smiled sadly at this. 'You already *have* a son with the name Francis. You have no need of another one.'

'Prithee do not speak of that wretch,' groaned Muriel. 'He broke Thomas's heart, and undoubtedly shortened his life. And now the scoundrel is coming here to claim the estate.'

'Did Thomas not disinherit him?'

'Aye, for a time, but then he changed his will back again – against my advice. My husband became foolish in his declining years, preferring to recall how delightful our son had been as a child and forgetting what kind of man he had become. As Shakespeare once said, Thomas "loved not wisely but too well".'

Sir Francis nodded in sympathy. Then he said: 'I suspect you are aware, my lady, that your son remains active in the rebel community. Indeed, he may be involved in a plot against the king.'

Muriel clenched her jaw at this news, but she did not seem surprised. 'You must stop him,' she said.

'We intend to. That is the reason we are here. I'd hoped to speak to Thomas – get his insight into a coded letter that was sent to your daughter's husband, Lord Monteagle. But perhaps the timing of our visit was not entirely unfortunate: if your son is on his way. It will give us a chance to confront him directly. Do you know when he is due?'

'This evening, I believe… But tell me about this letter. Do you have it with you? Perhaps I can help.'

Richard handed her the letter. 'This is a copy, my lady,' he explained. 'Lord Monteagle does not know I made it.'

'It is just as well,' said Muriel. 'I trust my son-in-law almost as little as I do my son – despite his declarations of loyalty. He is far too friendly with the papists. I worry constantly for the safety of my daughter Elizabeth.'

She perched a pair of eyeglasses on the bridge of her nose and studied the letter while Sir Francis explained: 'The number sequence is a simple substitution code. It reads: *My lord, on this date, find an excuse to retire to your country home, for we shall inflict a great blow upon our oppressors.*'

Muriel looked up sharply. 'A great blow?'

'Indeed. We have also located in Lambeth a store

of high-grade gunpowder smuggled in from France, which may be significant. Thus far we have identified three potential plotters, one of whom is your son.'

'By Minerva!' she cried. 'What the devil can he be playing at? Do you know when this *great blow* is to take place?'

'We do not. That crucial piece of information is contained here in the first part of the letter. Do you have any idea what it could mean?'

Muriel stared at it. 'Add the Candelabrum to the Seven Eyes of God…' She shook her head. 'It sounds like something Thomas would have known about. He was always reading about arcane Catholic signs and motifs. But I'm afraid it means nothing to me…' Then her gaze dropped to the bottom of the letter, and her mouth fell open. 'God-a-mercy!'

'What is it, my lady?'

'These symbols down here – I know what they mean, and none of it is good news.' She pointed to the circular, sun-like symbol in the bottom left corner. 'This Christogram is the insignia of a secret papist sect who believe in the violent overthrow of the Protestant state. As for the lamb, that represents holy sacrifice. In other words, blood that must be shed for the greater good. But this omega sign in the middle is the most ominous of all. It is shorthand for the apocalypse – meaning that the end of days is upon us. In other words, a great violence is to be carried out, and soon.'

Sir Francis frowned. 'By "soon" do you mean

before the end of the year?'

'I mean it could happen before the end of the week…'

Chapter 14

Mistress Anne's Secret

WHITEWEBBS, 1ST NOVEMBER 1605

Alice couldn't believe what Tresham was saying. 'I do *not* have the play, sir!' she insisted. 'Surely it was *you* who stole it!'

For a moment, Tresham simply stared at her. Then he cracked a smile, and not a pleasant one. 'I understand your game, lad. I know what you've done. You ratted on me, didn't you? You told Shakespeare about my plan. Then the two of you decided to hide the play and pretend it was stolen, just to keep it out of my hands.'

'That's not true,' protested Alice. 'I was about to steal the play, but then Mistress Anne invited me to have some food. I swear to you I was going to steal it straight afterwards.'

Tresham bit hard on his lower lip, as if fighting back the urge to strike her. 'So much for your fancy talk about believing in the restoration of the True Faith,' he muttered. 'I asked you to prove your loyalty with deeds not words, and you showed yourself to be just as spineless as the rest of them. Now where is it?'

'I told you, I don't have it.'

'You don't want to make an enemy of me, boy,' snarled Tresham. 'I advise you to hand it over right now.'

The door of the library suddenly swung open. 'Hand what over, Mr Tresham?' asked Anne Vaux.

Tresham looked irritated rather than perturbed by her appearance. 'Mr Shakespeare's missing play, if you must know,' he said. 'I believe Adam stole it.'

'Only because you asked me to,' blurted Alice. Then, glancing at Anne, she added sheepishly: '– although I didn't. Steal it, I mean.'

Anne's eyes narrowed in fury. Ignoring Alice, she went closer to Tresham and hissed: '*You* had the gall, in my house, to think of stealing from one of *my* guests. What possessed you?'

'I was planning to sell the play to raise funds, ma'am,' Tresham calmly replied.

'Funds for what?'

'We have plans to bring about the forceful restoration

of Catholicism in England.'

'It's true then,' said Anne through trembling lips. 'The rumours I've heard. You're going to kill the king…'

'We're going to correct a terrible error committed by an earlier king, Henry VIII. We're going to reverse seventy years of heresy and bring England back where it belongs, into the loving embrace of Rome. You should join us, my lady. You must see this is God's will.'

'Killing the king is not and never will be God's will,' said Anne. 'And you will never force this country back to the Roman Church at the point of a sword. It will happen by God's grace at the time of His choosing.'

'But *this* is that time, can you not see that?' shouted Tresham. 'James is a foreign king imposed upon this country by the hated Lord Cecil. He has little authority or popular support, even among the Protestants. If we delay, he will establish himself and, in time, be succeeded by his sons. By then it will be too late. *This* is the time, my lady. We must strike now, or be condemned to live as slaves forever.'

'I disagree, Mr Tresham. You need to have a little patience–'

'I am done with patience, Mistress!' thundered Tresham. 'Patience is a luxury I cannot afford. It is easy for someone like you to indulge in *patience* as you enjoy your comfortable life here in Whitewebbs. Cushioned by your wealth, you pay your recusancy fines and celebrate mass in your private chapel with your lute-playing priest. You soothe your conscience with prayers but you fail to lift a finger to stop the daily persecution of your Catholic brethren. I cannot be like you, Mistress Anne. I have fought for my faith, suffered in prison, come close to losing my head. I was disinherited by my father, reduced to near penury from the fines…'

'You know nothing of my life!' Anne shouted at him. 'You cannot say I haven't suffered. I have! But I will not add to the miseries of this world by stooping to violence. Nor will I offer shelter to those with violent aims. I want you to leave, Mr Tresham. Pack up your things and get out of here. I never want to see you again!'

With disdain upon his face, Tresham said: 'As you wish, Mistress. I was planning to leave today anyway. Enjoy your life here in your gilded cage, while the rest of us carry on the fight for your freedom and risk our heads on your behalf.' He bowed and withdrew.

When the door closed, Anne's dignified poise crumbled and she collapsed onto a chair and wept. 'Forgive me, Adam,' she sobbed. 'Forgive me for keeping company with such despicable men as Francis Tresham.'

'There is nothing to forgive, Mistress,' said Alice. 'You weren't to know what he was like.'

'That may have been wilful blindness on my part,' said Anne, wiping her eyes with a pocket handkerchief. 'I wanted to believe he was a good man – even after you told me about that brooch you saw him wearing… But it's not just my foolishness that's making me weep. It's something he said. He thinks of me as a happy woman living a life of ease, yet in this he is deeply mistaken. The truth is, my dear Adam, I am a wreck.'

'How so, Mistress?' asked Alice in surprise.

Anne's eyes were dry now, but ringed with deep lines of sorrow. 'You must promise to keep secret what I'm about to tell you,' she said. 'No one can know about it – no one at all.'

'I promise,' said Alice, wondering what she could be about to reveal.

'I am an unmarried woman, as you know,' said Anne, 'yet I have borne two children. I was obliged to give them away in their infancy. Not for my sake, you understand. I would have willingly endured any scandal, faced any punishment, to keep my two babes. It was something else that forced me to abandon them. I… I left them on the steps of Christ's Hospital in Newgate Street.'

An uncomfortable flutter ran through Alice when she heard this. Christ's Hospital was the orphanage where she and Richard had grown up. Her throat suddenly very dry, she asked: 'When… When did you leave them there, Mistress?'

'It was in that terrible year of the Spanish Armada, 1588,' Anne replied, once again close to tears. 'My three-year-old boy and my little girl, just eighteen months. Not a day goes by when I don't…' She could not continue.

Alice's whole body began to tremble. The dates matched. Richard would have been three in 1588, and she would have been a year and a half. 'Wh-What was it made you give them away?' she managed to ask.

'That's something I cannot say,' said Anne. 'It is altogether too painful...' She blew her nose, wiped her eyes and tried to recover some of her composure. 'Forgive me, my dear, for forcing this upon you. I felt an urgent need to unburden myself – to tell someone of the agony that sears my heart every single day. Perhaps it's for the best that it was *you* who heard my confession – a stranger, a travelling player, who I will likely never see again. Moreover you seem to me a kindly soul who will, I hope, not judge me too harshly.'

A knock at the door partially roused Alice from her state of dizzy confusion. Gus Philips blundered in without waiting to be ushered. 'Mistress Anne,' he bowed. 'I have come to bid you farewell...' Then he saw Alice. 'Ah, there you are! The carriages are in the yard. Everyone is waiting for you. Go quickly. We must leave at once if we are to make the nearest decent inn by nightfall.'

But Alice knew in her heart she could not leave. Not yet. She had too many questions.

Gus grew impatient. 'What is it, boy. Why are you still here?'

'I...' Alice tried to think of a plausible excuse. 'I cannot leave yet, Mr Philips,' she said, '– not while

Mr Shakespeare's manuscript remains missing. I must help with the search.'

'The devil you will! The script is gone. Father Henry's search yielded nothing, and the servants have all pleaded ignorance. Even Will is resigned to its loss. He says he'll rewrite it on our return to Southwark. Now come along.'

But Alice couldn't bear to go with him. Risking her continued status within the King's Men, she quietly insisted: 'I must stay and keep looking.'

Gus flushed a shade close to beetroot. He opened his mouth to bellow at her, when Anne intervened: 'Let the boy stay a little longer, Mr Philips. I'll furnish him with a fast horse from our stables. Rest assured, he'll reach Rushton Hall in good time for your performance.'

'Very well,' said Gus, glaring pointedly at Alice. 'We'll talk about this later.' He was about to sweep from the room when he stopped, remembering something. Turning to Anne, he said: 'You may be interested to hear, a guest has just arrived – a friend of Mr Tresham's.'

'Oh!' said Anne, surprised. 'And where is he now?'

'Mr Tresham has shown him into the withdrawing room. He seemed to be expecting him… I bid thee fare well, Mistress.'

'Oh, that Mr Tresham!' groaned Anne when Gus had gone. 'He invites his friends here as if he owns the place. I shall be very glad to see the back of him.'

Alice followed Anne out of the library, her heart still

bursting with questions, and determined not to let her out of her sight. They crossed the gallery and entered the withdrawing room. There was no sign of Tresham, but his guest was there, seated on Father Henry's vacated chair and sipping from his goblet of wassail.

He looked up when Anne entered, but did not rise to his feet.

'Well met, Mistress,' he muttered before taking another swig from Henry's cup.

The first thing Alice noticed about him was the bronze hook that protruded from the sleeve of his right arm. Then she saw his face, and got a huge shock.

'I am Mr Roberts,' he said. 'And I shall be resting up here for a day or two.'

Chapter 15

The Tunnel

LAMBETH–WESTMINSTER, 4ᵀᴴ NOVEMBER 1605

he two nightwatchmen stood on the river bank gazing down at Tom and Guido Fawkes. 'We're waiting for your answer,' said the ruddy-faced one. 'What is in those barrels?'

Calmly, Guido raised his head and smiled at them. 'Wine,' he said.

'Wine,' repeated the grey-bearded one as he smacked his heavy stick repeatedly against his palm. There was scorn in his voice, as if he didn't believe it. 'And why would you be transporting…' – he paused to count the barrels stacked in the boat – '...eight barrels of wine at this ungodly hour when all honest men are abed?'

'Honest men may be abed, sirrah,' chuckled Guido, 'but not the bishops, earls and barons of our Parliament. Across the river a party is in full swing at the House of Lords, and they have demanded more drink.'

Ruddy Face nodded, seemingly satisfied with this explanation, but Grey Beard remained suspicious. Slowly he descended the steps and joined them on the narrow jetty. He stepped into the boat and struck the nearest barrel with his stick. 'Open this up,' he said. 'I want to see what you've got in here.'

Guido's smile dimmed, leaving only the chilling emptiness of his stare. Tom saw his hand edge towards the hilt of his sword. *Did he plan to kill them?* Having seen how quick and deadly Guido could be, Tom didn't doubt he could dispatch both men before they were even fully aware of what was happening. Tom hated the thought of these innocent men getting slaughtered. But what could he do to save them?

'Come on! Be quick about it!' shouted Grey Beard, his eyes still fixed on the barrels.

With increasing alarm, Tom saw Guido start to draw his blade.

'We haven't time for this!' Tom suddenly blurted.

Grey Beard spun around, as Guido swiftly slid the sword back into his belt.

'What do you mean?' demanded Grey Beard.

'Lord Keyes,' babbled Tom – it was the first name that popped into his head. 'Lord Keyes will be extremely angry if his wine does not arrive soon. Of course we shall have to explain to him that it was you men of the nightwatch who were the cause of the delay by insisting on carrying out an inspection…'

Grey Beard didn't move from the boat. 'Is that so?' he growled.

Then Ruddy Face interjected: 'Come now, Mr Talbot. Let's not detain these gentlemen any longer in their urgent duty. I personally would sooner avoid coming between an angry lord and the refilling of his wine cup.'

With a final mistrustful glare at both of them, Grey Beard stepped out of the boat and returned to the bank. Soon, the two guardians of the night had disappeared into the fog.

Tom was expecting a tongue-lashing from Guido for his intervention. To his surprise he received praise. 'That was quick thinking, Claudio. I could have killed them, of course, but their disappearance would then have been noted, and we do not wish to attract the attention of the authorities when we are this close to achieving our goal.'

'Our goal being…?'

Guido flashed a grin. 'You'll find out soon enough.'

They climbed aboard the boat and Guido cast off. Taking an oar each, they steered into the glassy darkness of the river.

'Make for the north bank, close to the Parliament Stairs,' said Guido, pointing out a shadowy area to the left of a grand set of torchlit steps.

After ten minutes of steady rowing they reached the far side, and glided into a small quay. Guido leapt out of the boat and secured it to a mooring post, then said: 'Wait here and guard the barrels while I go and unlock the door and check the way is clear. I will return very soon.'

When Guido was gone, Tom climbed out of the boat and began pacing the quay, needing to get the blood flowing again through his cold, cramped legs. Above him loomed the towering grey walls of the Houses of Parliament. He wondered where Guido had gone. He'd mentioned unlocking a door – what door?

Suddenly Tom stopped, ears pricked. He'd heard something. It had sounded like a footstep.

'Mr Fawkes,' he whispered. 'Is that you?'

An urgent sound like a rush of breath lunged out of the darkness towards him. Something came swinging through the air. His head exploded with pain. He saw bright lights. Then nothing.

Tom awoke to find himself underwater. Everything was dim and grey down here at the bottom of the Thames, and the pressure of the water on top of his head was so great it hurt. His head had collapsed to somewhere just above his knees. He'd become entangled in river reeds and could scarcely move. With his body so compressed and pinioned, he had no hope of reaching the surface. He supposed he would just have to sit here until he drowned. Strangely, though, it didn't feel as if he was drowning, for he was still able to breathe – just. By pursing his lips, he could suck in meagre quantities of damp, watery air and send them down into his lungs. *Breathable water.* As an apprentice natural philosopher, Tom found this an intriguing concept. He would have liked to discuss his discovery with Sir Francis, had he been here.

At length, Tom's headache began to subside and his thoughts became more composed. He managed to raise his head and he saw, as he had already begun to suspect, that he was not underwater. He was on a chair in a room – an underground room close to the river, to judge from the chill dampness in his nostrils. The only illumination was a guttering rushlight fixed to a nearby wall. The 'river reeds' that bound his chest were, in fact, ropes holding him fast to the chair. He tried to pull at the ropes, but they were too thick, and if there was a knot in them it was out of reach at the back of the chair. How had he ended up in this sorry position? Memories slowly crawled from the fog in his mind. He'd been attacked by someone on the quayside while he was waiting for Guido to return. That someone must have imprisoned him here.

But why had he been with Guido? They'd been taking the gunpowder barrels somewhere – across the river to Westminster, that was it! And before that he'd been living in that house in Lambeth – Mr Roberts' house. Why? Because he'd been assigned to the task by Lord Cecil. So it was all Lord Cecil's fault that Tom now found himself tied up in a damp cellar at the mercy of a mysterious assailant. If it wasn't for Cecil, Tom would be living a comfortable and stimulating life assisting the great Sir Francis Bacon with his experiments.

How he missed his master… And he was sure Sir Francis missed him, too. But they had both accepted long ago that spying was a part of Tom's life. That didn't stop Sir Francis from feeling protective towards him, though. He recalled something he'd said to him just before he headed off to Lambeth. *When you are entering the territory of dangerous men, I always find it expedient to carry a concealed weapon.* Wise words from a wise man!

A concealed weapon… Of course! He'd said that after giving him a belt with a miniature knife hidden inside it. Looking down, Tom saw he was wearing the belt now. He flexed his fingers, which had become stiff with cold, and took off the belt. There, in a tiny sheath sewn into the belt's inner lining, was the knife. Tom pinched the carved bone handle, drew out the delicate blade and began to slice at the first rope. Though small, the blade was sharp, and immediately the rope began to fray. Within minutes, he had cut himself free.

He tried to rise, and toppled back into the chair, rocked by a wave of dizziness. The headache had returned. Tom squeezed his eyes shut for a moment and waited for the pain to pass. Then he tried again, this time more slowly. Once he was successfully on his feet, he examined his surroundings more carefully, searching for an exit. The walls, or what he could see of them in the dim orange flicker of the rushlight, were coated with black slime. There was no window, but there was a door. Tom stumbled over to it. He twisted its iron ring handle and pulled, then pushed. It wouldn't budge. It must have been bolted from the outside.

Frustrated, Tom plucked the rushlight from its wall bracket and began moving slowly around the room, searching without much hope for an alternative exit. On the floor by a pillar he found a lantern with a tallow candle inside. Using the rushlight, he lit the lantern, which provided a stronger, steadier glow. In its light he spotted, at the far end of the room, what looked like a knee-high wooden door set into the wall. Moving closer, he found, to his great disappointment, that it was nothing but a small pile of logs. In his anger, Tom kicked at the pile. Some of the logs rolled away, revealing a hole in the wall behind.

Tom got down on his knees and peered into the hole. To his surprise, he found himself looking along a tunnel that seemed to stretch well beyond the limits of the light thrown out by his lantern. An escape route? Maybe. Wherever it led, it had to be better than this horrid, slimy cellar. He had to bend his head and compress his body to squeeze through its tiny entrance.

But once inside, he found the tunnel relatively roomy, though the ceiling was too low for anything but crawling. The walls and ceiling of the tunnel were faced with brick and supported by wooden struts. The floor was cold, damp earth. Tom edged along slowly on his hand and knees while holding out the lantern before him. The deeper he went, the damper the tunnel became. Greenish slime covered the timber and brickwork. The floor became wet and soft, and his knees and hand sank inches into the sludge, slowing his progress. It may have been his imagination, but the walls and ceiling seemed to be closing in on him, as if the tunnel was gradually becoming narrower.

I should keep going, he told himself, shrugging off a growing anxiety. Things have to get better…

But they didn't.

Soon, the floor disappeared beneath a series of murky, smelly puddles. As he pushed through these, the splashes of his efforts echoed eerily off the walls. Tom had never felt so alone. The candle in his lantern flickered. He prayed it didn't go out.

The tunnel has to lead somewhere! He just had to keep going.

Before long, he could no longer see the floor. He was crawling through a river of fetid underground water. And it was rising. The further he went, the deeper he sank. The water was already up to his chest, and he had to hold his hand high and scrape his knuckles on the roof just to prevent the lantern from getting wet.

Eventually, the tunnel ended, and in the most

depressing way imaginable. There was no room at the end – no set of steps leading somewhere safe and dry. There was simply a solid stone wall. The wall was scarred with the marks of pick-axes. They looked freshly made. This tunnel to nowhere must have been recently built.

By now, the stinking black water had almost reached his neck and it chilled Tom deep inside his bones. He didn't think things could get any worse than this. He shivered violently, and water splashed onto the lantern. The candle sputtered and went out, shrouding him in complete darkness.

Oh yes, things could always get worse!

Determined not to give into fear or despair, Tom dumped the lantern, turned around and began swimming back up the tunnel. After what seemed like hours moving through pitch blackness, he glimpsed a faint flicker of the rushlight up ahead – the cellar, which he had been so eager to escape, now appeared to him as a blessed beacon of hope.

Ten minutes later, shivering uncontrollably, Tom pushed himself out of the hole and flopped exhausted on the cellar floor. He was coated from head to foot in black slime and could scarcely have looked human to anyone observing him.

As it turned out, someone *was* observing him, as he discovered to his shock when a boot connected violently with the side of his face. His ear went crack, and once again, a dark curtain fell over his mind.

Tom awoke from his stupor to find himself back on the wooden chair. This time, ropes bound his wrists to the chair's arms. He forced his head up, and through bleary eyes he saw a thin, hard face staring down at him.

Keyes!

He was back! Why had Tom ever assumed he wouldn't be.

'Tried to escape, didn't you?' he sneered, showing his long, yellow teeth. He was holding a large, very sharp knife at Tom's throat. 'I'll have to add that to your list of crimes, which is getting to be quite a long list, what with the spying, the assault, the slander, the lying, and now I've finally hunted you down, the escaping. What sort of punishment do you reckon you deserve for all that? Hmm?' He lowered the knife so it hovered just above Tom's right hand. 'A finger for each crime? I make that, let's see… five fingers in all. I could take them all off of the one hand, if you like, or some off of each. Tell me, boy, what shall it be?'

Chapter 16

The Banquet

RUSHTON HALL, 3ᴿᴰ NOVEMBER 1605

Richard looked out of the parlour window, alerted by the sound of wheels on gravel, and witnessed a convoy of wagons rolling into the courtyard.

He jumped up in surprise and glee. 'By my troth, it's the King's Men!' he shouted.

'The King's Men?' frowned Muriel. 'Why are *they* here? I didn't invite them.'

'Maybe your son did,' suggested Sir Francis. 'If he's setting up court here, he probably desires some entertainment.' He smiled. 'This is good news, my lady, for he would hardly be arranging theatrical events on the eve of a violent revolution. Despite your fears, this suggests the "apocalypse" is still weeks away.'

Richard ran out to greet his friends and fellow players. Gus, climbing out of the lead wagon, was astonished and delighted to see him. 'Richard! What are *you* doing here?'

'I could say the same about you, Mr Philips!' cried Richard as they clasped hands.

'But this is wonderful,' said Gus. 'You can take your old role of Claudio in *Measure for Measure*. We're performing it for Francis Tresham tomorrow evening.'

'I will if I can,' said Richard, 'although I am here on important government business.'

'As are we all, dear boy,' said Gus, tapping his nose. 'We're actually on a tour of the estates of England's leading papists. They're so busy watching our shows, they haven't got time to plot our country's destruction. All my idea, of course.'

'Actually, going to Whitewebbs was Adam's idea,' said John Heminges, joining them as they walked towards the house.

'Where *is* my brother?' Richard asked.

'Looking for my new play,' said a morose-looking Will Shakespeare, shuffling along behind them.

'You have a new play?' queried Richard.

'I did,' sighed Will. 'But now it's lost – or stolen. And I am obliged to write it again.'

'I hope for all our sakes it is merely lost,' said Gus. 'If it was stolen by the Earl of Derby's Men, or some other unsavoury troupe, they'll rush it onto the stage before you have time to rewrite it, and then it will be a devil of a job to prove that it's ours.' He glanced up to see a stern-looking Lady Muriel Tresham standing in the entrance to the house.

'To what do I owe the pleasure of this visit?' she said – though there was little evidence of pleasure in her voice.

'My lady,' bowed Gus. 'May I assume that you are the mother of Francis Tresham?'

'You may,' she said.

'Then I am most honoured to meet you. We are the King's Men, and your son generously invited us to perform a play here tomorrow evening.'

'And where is my son?' she asked.

'On his way. He left Whitewebbs shortly after we did, saying he had to meet first with some friends, but he hopes to be here by this evening.'

Francis Tresham reached Rushton Hall just after sunset, accompanied by eight friends. He led them into the lobby just as Muriel was emerging from the parlour.

'Mother!' he cried. 'How lovely to see you.' He extended his arms and whirled around in delight. 'And how wonderful to be back home after all these years. I cannot tell you how excited I was as we approached the gates. And now I'm here it's as if I was never away. The smell of the place. That little crack in the wainscot. I remember it all so clearly... I have missed being here.'

'In that case, it is a pity you didn't think to visit while your father was still alive,' said his mother coldly. 'Not once in five years did you cross that threshold. Yet here you are now, a week after his death, with all your friends and your travelling players, ready to host your revels... Your timing is, to say the least, insensitive.'

Tresham's smile withered. He rubbed his teeth back and forth across his lower lip, and for a moment it appeared as if he might become angry. But then he steadied himself and said: 'Mother, you know Father and I had our differences. He would not have welcomed me here.'

'He would have,' she murmured. 'All it would have taken was a simple apology – an acknowledgement of the wrong you did him, and of the debt you owed.'

'I acted according to my conscience. I have no reason to feel guilty...' Again, Francis became distracted by his surroundings. 'I remember this all so well. I'm glad you chose not to redecorate, Mother.'

'It was not a choice,' she said. 'We had no money for such things. Thomas had to pay out most of his fortune to save your neck. We very nearly had to sell up. Yet you never offered us a whisper of gratitude.'

This time she hit a nerve. Through gritted teeth, Tresham said: 'It is *you* who should be thanking *me*,

Mother. At least I am prepared to fight for our faith. If you and Father, along with others in our community, had backed the rebellion in 1601, then perhaps we could have won. And instead of paying out fines to these monsters, they'd be dead and we'd be living in a Catholic England.'

'How long will you be staying?' asked Muriel, her voice like glass.

'For as long as it pleases me,' answered her son. 'Since the estate is now mine, why should I ever leave?' As an afterthought, he added: 'And of course you are welcome to remain here, too, Mother.'

'How very gracious of you,' she scowled. 'Now if you and your friends will excuse me, I must go and see Cook about supper.'

That evening, everyone gathered in the Great Hall for a banquet before a roaring fire. Among the dishes served were roast boar with mustard, roast larks, roasted swans with cloves, venison stew, eel pies with garlic purée, sugared jumbles and honeyed fruits. There were eighteen present at the feast: Francis Tresham, Lady Muriel Tresham, Sir Francis Bacon, the senior members of the King's Men (Gus Philips, John Heminges, Richard Burbage, Will Shakespeare, Henry Condell, Robert Armin and Richard Fletcher) and Tresham's friends (John Wright, Thomas Wintour, Robert Wintour, Thomas Percy, Thomas Bates, John Grant, Ambrose Rookwood and Sir Everard Digby).

Tresham devised a seating plan that interspersed his friends with the King's Men, so as to avoid (he said) two cliques and two separate conversations emerging. 'I want us to dine as a single body of friends,' he told them, which meant, in effect, that everyone found themselves seated next to a stranger. Tresham's friends, it turned out, had little interest in the theatre, and the King's Men were not hugely concerned about the plight of the English Catholics (which Tresham's friends were). As a result, conversation was stilted.

Towards the end of the feast, Tresham rose to his feet and toasted the King's Men. 'We are privileged,' he said, 'to welcome among us this fine body of players. The King's Men have been delighting audiences at the Globe in Southwark for many years now, and they are, without question, the most talented players of our age. As for their playwright, Mr William Shakespeare, he is commonly acknowledged to be a genius, whose words will be spoken on stages for centuries to come. It therefore pains me to say this, but say it I must…'

There was an uncomfortable shuffling of chairs around the table, as people waited uneasily for what was to follow.

'Since our current monarch ascended to the throne two years ago,' Tresham continued, 'the King's Men have displayed an attitude towards him that I can only describe as grovelling and fawning – an attitude that I and many others find utterly abhorrent. Having obtained the king's patronage, they are now, both

in name and deed, *his* men. The plays they perform
serve only to promote his rule. Plays like *Julius Caesar*
and *Hamlet* disparage any attempt to unseat a ruler,
however cruel or tyrannical that ruler might be. And
the saddest part of it is that the writer of these plays –
the great William Shakespeare – is himself a Catholic.
He comes from a well-known family of recusants. Yet
he chooses to deny these noble roots and instead acts
as a sycophantic courtier to a ruthless Protestant king.'

Robert Armin, Henry Condell and Richard
Burbage had begun banging on the table with their
knives in protest long before Tresham had finished
this speech. John Heminges tried to point out that
both *Caesar* and *Hamlet* were written during the
reign of Elizabeth. As for Gus, he could only stare at
Tresham, his jaw slack with astonishment, a stream
of drool mixed with venison gravy dribbling down
his chin. Richard guessed what he was thinking: *Have
we been tricked? Did Tresham invite us here to perform – or
to be insulted?*

Will Shakespeare sat through it all in silence, calmly
staring at his trencher. However, the other members
of the troupe were more vocal. 'Untrue!' cried Armin,
Condell and Burbage. 'Slander!'

'Do you really think so?' Tresham challenged
them. 'Then what say you to this?' With a flourish,
he produced from beneath his cloak a thick bundle of
pages. 'Here is Mr Shakespeare's latest play, *Macbeth*.'

This provoked shocked gasps from the King's Men.

'*You* have it! But how? And why?' cried Gus.

Tresham smiled. 'I happened to overhear your conversation at the Mermaid Tavern four days ago, when Mr Shakespeare described his play. It sounded like yet another piece puffing up King James and his dreadful dynasty. At Whitewebbs, I saw my chance to do something about it. I tried to persuade young Adam from your troupe to steal it for me. Whether he ever planned to do so, I know not. It didn't matter, because the play was stolen by someone else. Earlier, I'd written to my hook-handed friend Robert Catesby, telling him about the play. Catesby, who was coming to Whitewebbs the following day, decided to steal it too. He arrived at the house an hour before anyone noticed him, and crept into Mr Shakespeare's bedroom through an open casement, where he found the manuscript on a table. He handed it to me as I was leaving Whitewebbs. Heaven be praised! I told Adam that my plan was to sell it for money. But that was a lie. This play is far too dangerous to be performed, even by another troupe...' Tresham strode over to the hearth, and lifted up the manuscript. 'In the new, Catholic England we are about to create, there will be no place for heretical works like this,' he said.

'No!' screamed Gus, as Tresham tossed the entire play onto the fire.

Richard watched in horror as the flames greedily caressed the pages, turning their edges a crispy brown. Without thinking about the consequences, he leapt from his bench and dived towards the hearth in an effort to salvage what he could of Will's work from the blaze. But before he could get there, he was seized from behind by two of Tresham's friends and dragged back to the table. Unable to free himself from their grip, he was forced to watch as the flames leapt and crackled, and the pages, dense with handwritten text, began to blacken and crumble to embers and smoke. He hated to imagine the thoughts of Will Shakespeare in that moment.

'I did not invite you here to perform,' Tresham told them, 'but to bear witness to a changing order.'

'And when is this new order due to begin?' asked Sir Francis Bacon.

'You will have to watch and wait for it. But what you will not be able to do is warn anyone.'

Tresham gave a nod, and, as one, each of his friends drew a dagger from his belt and pointed it at the man to his left.

The reason for Tresham's seating plan was now horribly clear. Sir Francis Bacon and the King's Men had become Tresham's prisoners.

Chapter 17

Catesby Takes Control

WHITEWEBBS, 1ST NOVEMBER 1605

Alice darted into the shadow of a large iron candle stand, praying Robert Catesby hadn't seen her. For it was certainly him, the man who had tortured her for three days during her imprisonment at Bradenstoke Hall. She would never forget that face – though it had aged greatly in just two and a half years, and his flesh was now tinged with a sickly pallor. Yet even in his weakened state, the fact of his presence scared her – he should not have survived in that forest a single night with such a wound.

She pressed herself deeper into the shadows. *Catesby*. The very word made her shudder. During those three terrible days at Bradenstoke she had come to view him as the devil incarnate. That he was here, still alive, seemed further proof of his almost supernatural evil.

'You have no right to demand my hospitality, Mr Roberts,' Anne told him. 'I refuse to allow my house to be used as a sanctuary for fugitive papists. I don't care if you are Mr Tresham's friend. Mr Tresham is no longer welcome here, and neither are you.'

Catesby put down his goblet. He rose to his feet and approached the hearth. Alice, fearing he might see her, edged out of sight behind a wall tapestry. He crouched down by the fire and placed the sharp tip of his hook-hand into the flames. Alice watched as the metal gradually turn pinked in the heat – it was an unnerving yet mesmerising sight, When he rose again, and turned to face Anne, Catesby had a matchlock pistol in his left hand.

'My good woman,' he drawled, 'you clearly don't understand me. I wasn't asking for your hospitality. I was merely informing you that I shall be staying here a while.'

With the glowing tip of his hook, he lit the pistol's slow-burning hemp cord.

Anne paled, but kept her composure. 'My guards will eject you,' she said.

'Guards? You mean those fellows at the gate who

my men captured and locked up in the stable? They won't be bothering us.'

He returned to his chair and leaned back, spreading his limbs in a lordly fashion as if *he* was the owner of the house and Anne was his servant. 'Now, my good woman, will you fetch me some supper? I've ridden all the way from Lambeth and my belly needs filling.'

'I will *not*,' she said firmly.

Casually, Catesby turned the muzzle of his pistol on Father Henry's beloved lute, which was leaning up against the virginal. He began to press down on the firing button. 'Wait!' cried Anne. 'I'll do it. By Minerva, I'll bring you your wretched supper!'

'Excellent, madam. Be quick about it.'

Anne departed the room, and Alice left the refuge of the tapestry and followed her. She moved swiftly, keeping her head down, making it through the door just as it was closing. Catesby must have thought her a servant, for he failed to even look at her. The immediate danger was over. Yet for as long as he remained here, she would have to be very careful. He would remember her, and would want his revenge.

Anne was halfway down the corridor when Alice caught up with her.

'He has brought men here,' Anne muttered as they walked. 'I wonder how many. I must find Henry.'

They arrived at the lobby, and there was Henry, coming down the stairs. 'Thank the Lord, you're safe,' he said, rushing towards them and embracing Anne.

'The guards are missing. The servants are in a panic. I've just seen from an upstairs window, there are armed men in the grounds.'

'It's Mr Roberts' doing,' said Anne. 'He's a friend of Francis Tresham's, who arrived here a short while ago and has ensconced himself in the withdrawing room. He has a pistol.'

'Mercy!' whispered Henry.

'Perhaps we can escape,' suggested Alice. 'We can take the horses in the stables.'

Henry shook his head. 'He has men guarding the stables and the outer gates.'

'Then we are trapped,' sighed Anne.

'What does this Roberts fellow want?' asked Henry.

'Food,' said Anne. 'I was about to go and see Cook.'

'You do that,' said Henry. 'Meanwhile I shall go and speak with the man. Maybe I can reason with him.'

'Be careful,' pleaded Anne. 'He's dangerous – more animal than man.'

She watched him leave, anxiety etched on her brow. Then she turned and began walking towards the kitchen.

Alice lingered, watching her go, her heart filled with turmoil. She didn't know when, if ever, she and Anne might find themselves alone again.

'My lady,' she called.

Anne turned. 'What is it?'

'I know you have much on your mind, and this is probably not the best time. But... there is something

I must tell you. It's been weighing on me ever since we had that conversation in the library – about the children you were forced to give away.'

'What of them?' asked Anne with a distracted frown.

'You said you sent them to Christ's Hospital in Newgate Street.'

'Aye. So?'

'I grew up in that orphanage. I… I may have known them.'

Anne became very still. She stared at Alice for a long time without saying anything, just thinking. Then, quietly, she said: 'Pray, tell me if you think you remember them.'

At that moment, the obvious thing for Alice to do would have been to open up and tell her everything: that she was, in fact, a girl, that she had an older brother, and that she and Richard might well be Anne's long-lost children. What stopped her was a deep-seated rage, which had built up over the years – a rage at the woman who had so callously abandoned them on the steps of that orphanage. All the hardship and suffering that had followed was, she had assured herself many times, down to her. Alice couldn't simply run into the arms of such a woman, bestow upon her the title of *mother*, and act as if all was forgiven.

'I shall tell you what I know,' Alice said coolly. 'But first, please answer me something: why did you give your children away?'

Anne took a deep breath, and her eyes filled with

sudden tears. 'That is a secret I must take with me to my grave,' she replied. 'It is the curse of my life, the cross I must bear.' Alice thought she glimpsed a vast guilt and despair in Anne as she said these words. It appeared that this lady had not forgiven herself for what she'd done, and maybe never would. The painting of the children, the untouched toys in the cabinet, were there to constantly remind her of what she had lost, and to punish her for what she had done.

'So?' said Anne. 'Do you remember them?'

What to do? Should she tell her?

No. At least not yet. Only when Anne was prepared to divulge her own big secret, would Alice consider revealing hers...

'I believed for a moment that I did,' said Alice, 'but now I'm not sure. Forgive me. Perhaps later, when we have more time, you can tell me about them. It may spark a memory.'

Anne blinked back a tear. 'You are right, Adam. We can talk about this later. Right now we must order up some supper for our hungry guest.'

A short while later, Anne carried a tray of meat pies and ale back to the withdrawing room. Alice followed several steps behind her. She had already decided to wait outside while Anne delivered the food, to avoid being seen by Catesby. As Anne was approaching the room, Henry emerged through the door, looking frustrated. 'I cannot get any information out of the man about his intentions,' he reported. 'All he says is he's hungry and wants food.'

'Well, here it is,' said Anne. 'Maybe once his stomach is full, he'll be more forthcoming.'

Before she could reach the door, however, it swung open again and Catesby burst into the corridor, his eyes darting about suspiciously. 'I heard voices out here,' he growled. 'Is that my food?' Then he spotted Alice, who hadn't been able to scoot out of sight in time. His face darkened. '*You!*' he snarled, aiming his pistol at her. 'I remember you!'

Chapter 18

The Undercroft

WESTMINSTER, 4TH NOVEMBER 1605

The knife blade closed in on the forefinger of Tom's right hand. 'How about we start with this one?' suggested Mr Keyes. 'You won't be so handy with a sword when that finger's gone, will you?' He cackled, an arid, goat-like sound.

Tom strained at the rope binding his wrist to the chair arm, trying desperately to keep his hand away from the blade. But Keyes' knots were good and tight. There was no give in the rope. With his left hand, Keyes forced Tom's hand flat, palm downwards. The knife descended until Tom could feel its cold sharpness pressing into the skin of his finger, just beneath the lower knuckle, close to the hand. A dribble of blood oozed out as the blade began to cut.

Tom tried to swallow, but his mouth was utterly dry. He tried to ready himself, for his world was about to bloom with pain, and his life after that – if life there was – didn't bear thinking about... How would he eat, dress, fight or feel without fingers? How would he hold someone's hand? He didn't want to live like that – mutilated. It would be better to bleed to death here in this cellar.

As the pain swelled, Tom's vision blurred. Strange sounds filled the air. *Was that the creak of a door?* He sensed sudden movement – a flash of silver. *What was going on?* The pain in his finger eased as the knife fell away and clattered to the floor. He glanced up to see Keyes leering at him, his mouth wet with blood, and six inches of steel blade protruding from his chest. Something juddered in Keyes' eyes, like a dying candle – then it was gone and he collapsed.

Behind him stood Guido Fawkes. He extracted his sword from Keyes' back and wiped off the blood on the slain man's shirt.

'God's Teeth!' hissed Guido, as his sword sliced through Tom's bonds. 'That man must hate you. It is fortunate I arrived here in time!'

'Wh-What happened? How did you find me?'

'Pure fortune,' said Guido. 'I returned to the boat and you were gone. After searching the precincts of the palace, I gave up and unloaded the barrels myself. After that, I came here, to the house of my friend Thomas Percy, for some refreshment. If I hadn't spied the light burning in the cellar, I would never have come down here.'

Freed of his restraints, Tom staggered to his feet, then fell against a pillar, his legs shaking uncontrollably.

'You're in a bad state,' said Guido, his brow crinkling in sympathy. He handed Tom a handkerchief. 'Here, this will stop the blood.'

Tom clamped it to his injured finger. The gash was deep and painful.

'Why are you covered in black sludge?' Guido asked him.

'Tried to escape… down the tunnel,' Tom croaked. He nodded at the hole in the back wall of the room.

'Ah, that,' said Guido. 'That took a lot of time and sweat to build.'

'Why did you build it?' Tom asked. 'It leads nowhere.'

'We had to abandon it,' said Guido. 'Being this close to the Thames, it became waterlogged. And when we finally reached the House of Lords, the foundations were too thick to break through.'

Tom, still in a mild state of shock, struggled to understand. 'Why did you need to reach the House of Lords?'

And then, like a hammer blow, he realised: 'You were

going to blow it up, with the gunpowder.'

Guido nodded. 'That was our intention.'

'While the king was in there.'

'Aye, during the State Opening of Parliament.'

'So not only the king then. You were planning to kill all the peers of the realm.'

'I call it the *decapitation strategy*,' smiled Guido. 'The entire Protestant establishment wiped out in one big, beautiful explosion…'

Tom fell silent, trying to absorb the monstrous ambition of such a plan.

But the foundations had proved too thick…

'So if the plan failed, why are we still moving the gunpowder here?'

'The plan hasn't failed, it's just changed. Here, let me show you…'

Guido turned and headed out of the cellar. After a final glance at Keyes, the bloody death-grin still spread across his face, Tom followed. They ascended a gloomy set of steps that led to the ground floor of a small, but comfortably furnished house. 'This place belongs to my friend, Thomas Percy,' explained Guido. 'He bought it because of its location, next door to Parliament – perfect for our plans, until we hit the impenetrable barrier of those foundations.'

He led Tom out of the house and into a cobbled square. Percy's home was dwarfed by its neighbour, the House of Lords, a grand edifice of arched windows and soaring buttresses that occupied one entire side of the square.

Tom followed Guido to a discreet entrance, tucked down a small alleyway. A set of spiral stone steps led them into a pitch dark, echoey room. Guido lit a lantern, and Tom saw they were in a spacious undercroft, its vaulted ceiling held up by two long, parallel rows of pillars stretching back more than thirty yards.

'We had a stroke of fortune,' said Guido. 'By God's grace, last March, Percy managed to rent out this undercroft. It's directly beneath the chamber of the House of Lords.'

They walked between the pillars to the far end. In the glow of Guido's lantern, Tom saw a gigantic mound of fagots and billets – the product of all those hours of labour by himself and Kit – piled up against the wall.

'So *this* is where you've been taking it all,' Tom gasped. 'But this looks like far more than Kit and I made…' Then he glimpsed, deep inside the pile, something that didn't look like a fagot or a billet. He pushed aside some of the stick bundles and wood to take a closer look. It was a barrel.

'The barrels of gunpowder… You've already added them to the pile?'

'Aye,' said Guido. 'They were the last of them.'

'The *last* of them?'

'I've been smuggling gunpowder barrels across the river and down here for the past eight months,' explained Guido, '– usually just two or three at a time.'

'So how many barrels are there altogether?' Tom asked.

'Thirty-six. That should do the job, and some.'

Guido didn't seem to notice, or be bothered by, the stricken look on Tom's face. Four nights ago, at the Woolpack, Sir Francis had described the destructive power of eight barrels of gunpowder. He estimated it would be enough to obliterate everything, including stone walls, within 30 feet, and would cause major structural damage to anything within 360 feet.

But that was eight barrels...

With thirty-six barrels, the devastation would cover an area four and a half times bigger. The explosion would destroy not only the House of Lords, but much of the Palace of Westminster – the Abbey, Westminster Hall, St Stephen's Chapel...

The sallow light of the lantern played upon Guido's face, deepening its shadows, brightening his teeth and eyes. He was smiling, as usual, but Tom could only see the huge void that lay behind that smile – the complete absence of human feeling.

'Tomorrow morning,' said Guido Fawkes, 'the king and all his lords will gather in the chamber above for the State Opening of Parliament, and I plan to blow every single one of them to kingdom come.'

Act Four

Chapter 19

The Triangular Lodge

RUSHTON HALL, 4TH NOVEMBER 1605

Richard awoke to a soft, steady sound of clunks and creaks. Gradually he came to recognise it as footsteps on a wooden floor. There was a pattern to it that went like this: *Clunk clunk creak clunk pause… clunk creak clunk clunk pause… clunk clunk creak clunk pause... clunk creak clunk clunk pause…*

He blinked a few times. Pale grey dawn light leaked into his eyes from a nearby casement. *Where was he?* Then he saw the figure of Sir Francis Bacon moving slowly back and forth through his field of vision – it had been his pacing that had woken him – and he remembered. He and Sir Francis were prisoners – cell mates – in one of the upper-floor rooms of Rushton Hall. Gus Philips, John Heminges, Will Shakespeare and the other King's Men were being held elsewhere in the house.

The footsteps stopped. 'You're awake!' said Sir Francis, who was fully dressed and looking as bright and alert as a sparrow.

'Aye,' croaked Richard and he struggled into a more upright position on his narrow bed. The room's other bed was neatly remade. The only hint that Sir Francis had ever lain there was the slight depression in the pillow.

'Why are we being held here, do you suppose?' Sir Francis asked – no *Good mornings* or *How did you sleeps?* from him! He looked like he'd been wrestling with this question for most of the night.

'Tresham didn't really explain,' said Richard. 'He just said he wanted us to "bear witness to a changing order".'

'To *bear witness*,' nodded Sir Francis. 'Well remembered. That was the exact phrase he used. But what does it mean?'

'I suppose it means, to say that something is true, that it happened.'

'Precisely!' said Sir Francis, nodding ever more vigorously. 'Once Tresham and his papist friends have overthrown King James and his ministers, they'll need to get the public to accept what's happened and what's true, which is that England is, once again, a Catholic country. If they can get popular support for this, half the battle is won.'

'So where do we come in?' asked Richard.

'You're going to be their heralds, proclaiming the good news. They'll want Shakespeare to write plays glorifying the new regime, which the King's Men can perform at venues around the country.' Sir Francis had begun his pacing again: *clunk clunk creak clunk pause... clunk creak clunk clunk pause...* 'Such is the power of Shakespeare's words, especially when spoken by the talented Mr Burbage, that the hearts of audiences are bound to be moved and their spirits uplifted. Word will quickly spread through the inns, taverns and public squares of our towns and cities. The people of England will come to realise the catastrophic mistake they made seven decades ago when they turned their backs on the Mother Church, and they'll welcome their country's restoration to the family of Catholic nations.'

'Do you really believe all that?' asked Richard.

'No, of course not,' said Sir Francis. 'But Tresham believes it, and that's why you're here.'

'And you? Why are *you* here?'

Sir Francis paused in his pacing. 'By accident,' he said. 'Tresham didn't know I was coming. But I suspect he's pleased to have me all the same, and will want me to "bear witness" along with the rest of you. Imagine the impact on the people when they hear that Sir Francis Bacon, renowned philosopher and friend of King James, has given his support to this papist uprising...'

'When do you suppose the attack on the king will happen?'

'Soon,' said Sir Francis. 'They won't want to keep us confined like this for long. People of our status cannot simply disappear without causing a stir, so they know they don't have much time. I was hoping we had a few weeks before they launch their "great blow", but it may only be a matter of days.'

'Then we must get out of here, so we can warn Lord Cecil and the king,' said Richard, getting out of bed.

'That might not be so easy,' said Sir Francis. 'The door to our room is locked, and there's always a guard out there. They work in three-hour shifts, with no time in between.' By now he had resumed his pacing. *Clunk creak clunk clunk pause... clunk clunk creak clunk pause...Clunk clunk creak clunk pause... clunk creak clunk clunk pause...*

It clearly helped Sir Francis's thinking process to pace about like this with his head lowered and his hands clasped behind his back. As Richard got dressed, he listened to the philosopher moving slowly one way, then the other, over the same patch of floor. *Clunk creak clunk clunk pause... clunk clunk creak clunk pause...*

He couldn't help noticing that there was always a creak on the second step when Sir Francis moved from left to right, and on the third step when he moved from right to left. After buttoning his tunic, Richard glanced down at the area of the wooden floor that creaked. It looked identical to the rest. He knelt by it and stared, watching closely each time Sir Francis's foot creaked.

Noticing Richard's sudden interest in the floor, Sir Francis stopped pacing. 'What is it?' he asked.

'Something is causing that creak,' said Richard, 'but the floorboards look new, and the nails appear perfectly sound.'

Sir Francis, always excited by a mystery, immediately joined Richard on the floor. 'I see what you mean,' he said after giving it a close examination. 'Perhaps there's a gap in the joists underneath, though I don't understand how; the nails are spaced just a foot apart, as they are everywhere else on this floorboard.' He pushed down hard on the floorboard with the heel of his hand. There was a slight but noticeable give. Yet he'd placed his hand between the nails, right over the joist, where the floor should have been at its most solid.

'Perhaps the nails aren't connected to anything,' suggested Richard.

Sir Francis peered at them more closely. 'There is something odd about these nails,' he murmured, and he ran a finger across the embedded head of one of them. 'Feel that,' he said.

Richard did so. To his surprise, he couldn't feel anything beneath his finger. He tried rubbing the area several times. 'It's perfectly smooth here,' he said. 'It's as if there is no nail.'

'That's because there isn't,' said Sir Francis. 'Nor here,' he added, indicating the other nail. 'These nail heads have been painted on.'

'But why would anyone do that?'

'Maybe to disguise the fact that there's a space under this floor. It reminds me of the work of Nicholas Owen.'

'Who's he?'

'A builder of priest holes…'

'You think there may be a priest hole under here?'

'I can't see any other reason for these painted-on nail heads, can you? Look, there are more of them on the adjacent floorboards.' Sir Francis spread out his hands, palms down, and ran them more widely across the area. 'There should be a cleft here somewhere – the edge of a trapdoor.'

Richard helped him, and eventually they found a very fine seam, about two feet long, running perpendicular to the floorboards. 'I would never have spotted that,' Richard said, 'because it's hidden by the knots in the wood.'

'Classic Nicholas Owen,' remarked Sir Francis. 'You won't hear me say this in front of Lord Cecil, but I rather admire the man's artistry. He specialises in creating perfectly disguised entrances, just like this one, designed to fool the eye. I would lay money on this being one of his.'

'If it hadn't been for the creaking sound you made, we would never have found it,' said Richard. He was already thinking of how they could make use of this discovery. 'Perhaps if there *is* a priest hole under here, we could hide in it, and when the guards come in, they'll find the room empty and assume we've escaped. They'll dash off in search of us, hopefully leaving the door open.'

'It's a wonderful plan,' said Sir Francis. 'But first we must work out how to open the trapdoor.'

It didn't take long for them to discern a wooden ring inlaid within the floor very close to the trapdoor edge. Again, it was their fingers that found it, not their eyes, for the ring was perfectly disguised within the grain of the wood.

The ring was attached to the floor by means of a tiny, almost invisible hinge. By scrabbling at it with his nails, Richard was able to raise the ring clear of its housing so that it stood proud of the floor. He yanked it upwards and, with a sharp squeak and a puff of dust, the trapdoor opened.

Sir Francis and Richard peered into the tiny, cramped-looking space beneath the trapdoor.

'Built for a very small priest,' said Richard disappointedly. 'I'd struggle to fit inside there on my own, let alone both of us.'

'Wait a moment,' said Sir Francis, kneeling down close to the edge and peering in. 'This isn't a hole, it's a tunnel.'

He was right! At the bottom of the hole, Richard discerned an opening on one side that looked very much like the start of a cramped passage between the floor and the ceiling below.

Good news! This wasn't a priest hole, it was a priest's escape route!

Richard led the way. He squeezed himself into the hole, then ducked down inside the constricted passage. It was a tight fit and didn't smell very pleasant. A horrid thought crossed his mind that he might get stuck in here. It would be a squalid end indeed!

'I'm right behind you,' whispered Sir Francis. Richard heard the trapdoor slamming shut behind him, and the darkness became total. 'That'll confuse the guards,' Sir Francis giggled. Then he added in a more sombre tone: 'I do hope this tunnel leads somewhere, for I'm not at all sure I can reopen that trapdoor.'

Richard moved himself forwards by pushing with his hands against the walls on either side. Progress was slow, but he was soon cheered by vague glimmerings of light visible at the far end, and a faint hint of fresh air. Several yards on, he found himself leaning over a square-shaped brick shaft. Daylight shone up from below. It was a garderobe shaft set into the house's outside wall – a disused one he hoped! A rope attached to the tunnel roof hung down the shaft. It must have been placed there so that escaping priests could climb down it and make their getaway.

Richard took a deep breath, seized hold of the rope and began clambering down the shaft, slowing and controlling his descent with his feet. Very soon he was out of the shaft and in the open air, dangling over some bushes and grass growing against the wall. The drop to the ground from this height was short and relatively easy. Seconds later, Sir Francis tumbled down next to him. He immediately sprang up, clutching his bottom and yelping in pain. He turned to examine the prickly shrub he'd just landed in. 'Genus Ulex, from the family *Leguminosae*,' he groaned. 'Commonly known as gorse.'

'You have my sympathies,' said Richard, 'but we ought to make haste before someone spots us. Which way do you suggest we go?'

Sir Francis, still rubbing his tender rear, scanned their surroundings. To the east lay Rushton village, where they were almost certain to be seen. To the south and west were the estate's formal gardens – shrub-lined pathways and square beds of flowers. Venturing into there would leave them highly visible to anyone watching from a window.

'That way,' said Sir Francis, pointing west-north-west towards an open patch of ground rising to a forest beyond. The sight of the forest cheered Richard, for he was naturally drawn to woodland. They began running towards it, and although their speed was limited by Sir Francis's short legs and the rough terrain of the meadow, they made good progress. Before long,

Richard saw they were approaching something rather curious. It was, at first sight, nothing more than an angular shape standing atop a low ridge at the edge of the forest. But the closer they went, the more curious and strange it became.

When they finally reached it, they stared in breathless wonderment at the structure, which Richard immediately decided was the strangest building he'd ever seen.

'This,' gasped Sir Francis when he could finally speak, 'must be the Triangular Lodge.'

'The Triangular Lodge,' echoed Richard. 'It is well named, for it is perfectly triangular.'

And it was. The building had three walls, and seen from above it would have appeared as a triangle on the ground. There were also triangular roof gables on each of its sides, and smaller triangles set within its windows and walls.

'Sir Thomas often spoke of this place,' said Sir Francis, 'and I regret I never managed to see it while he was still alive. He built it, you know, as a celebration of his faith. The Holy Trinity – Father, Son and Holy Spirit – is everywhere in this building, represented by the number three. There are three walls, each exactly 33 feet long. Each wall has three windows and is topped by three gables. Inside, there are three floors, with three rooms on each floor. And you see those Latin texts carved into the walls up there, just beneath the gables? Each one is 33 letters long.'

Sir Francis walked closer to the entrance. He pointed out an inscription above it, which read: TRES TESTIMONIUM DANT. 'There are three that bear witness,' he translated. 'There's that phrase again!'

'That's from the Bible, isn't it?' said Richard.

'The Gospel of St John, Chapter 5, Verse 7,' confirmed Sir Francis. 'It refers to the Holy Trinity, but it's also a private family joke. You see, Lady Muriel always called Sir Thomas 'Good Tres' in her letters to him. So it could be translated as *Tresham bears witness…*'

Richard was astounded by all this, but at the same time he could not ignore a faint drumbeat of fear that had started up within him – an instinctive sense of impending danger. He looked back towards Rushton Hall, but could see no one approaching from that direction. Still, he'd learned to trust this feeling since his days in the forest.

'This is all very extraordinary,' he said to Sir Francis, 'but I think we should go now. This place feels quite exposed. Also, we need to get back to London… Sir Francis?'

The philosopher wasn't listening. His attention was focused on something that had caught his eye right at the top of the building. He was murmuring under his breath.

'Are you alright sir?' asked Richard.

Sir Francis suddenly turned to him. 'Add the Candelabrum to the Seven Eyes of God. That's what the Monteagle letter said, wasn't it?'

'Aye, sir, but...'

'Look!' Sir Francis pointed to one of the gables high above them. 'The Candelabrum, see?'

Richard looked, and saw a seven-branched candlestick holder carved into the stonework.

Then Sir Francis pointed to another gable. 'And there are the Seven Eyes of God.'

Craning his neck and squinting once more, Richard saw what at first looked like seven raised circular bumps arranged on a circle inside a heptagon. Looking more closely, he saw that the seven bumps were, in fact, eyes, complete with lids, pupils and irises.

'There's a number above it,' said Richard.

'There are numbers above both of them,' said Sir Francis. 'Read them out will you?'

After more squinting and staring, Richard made the figures out: 'Above the Candelabrum is 3898, and above the Seven Eyes of God is... 3509.'

Sir Francis began to giggle, and his giggle soon turned into a laugh. He laughed for so long and with such abandon that Richard began to get worried.

'Are you alright, sir?'

'All this time,' Sir Francis eventually managed to splutter. 'All this time, I've been thinking the code was something mystical that only a scholar steeped in obscure Catholic lore could possibly unravel. But in the end it's just simple mathematics. When it says *Add the Candelabrum to the Seven Eyes of God*, it means "add together two numbers". This is fantastic! Not only can we now solve the code and work out the date of the "great blow", we can also say for certain who wrote the letter.'

'How can we know that?'

'Because there are only three people alive who know the carvings on this lodge well enough to concoct such a code. They are Lady Muriel; her son-in-law Lord Monteagle, who, Sir Thomas told me, displayed a deep interest in the project; and Francis Tresham. We can discount Lady Muriel, for it was clear from her reaction yesterday that she had no knowledge of the plot. As for Monteagle, he could not have written the letter to himself. Which leaves…'

'Which leaves Tresham,' gasped Richard. 'He must have realised that Monteagle was the only person in the world, apart from his mother, who would know what the different symbols signified. It's the perfect code.'

Sir Francis nodded in agreement. 'And it is our fortune to have stumbled upon the key to breaking it. So let's get to work…' His brow furrowed as he began his calculations: '3898 plus 3509 is… 7407, I believe. What did the letter say next?'

Richard no longer had the letter – it had been taken from him last night. But he remembered the first part word for word. 'It said subtract 4000.'

'Very well… 7407 less 4000 gives us 3407. And then?'

'Multiply by the difference between the Hen and the Pelican.'

'The Hen and the Pelican…' Sir Francis began jogging around the building, keeping his eyes on the gables. On the north side, he found what he was looking for. 'See up there,' he pointed out to Richard when he'd caught up with him. Richard peered upwards and saw a carving of what looked like a hen with her chicks. On another gable was a bird that he might have recognised as a pelican, had he known what a pelican looked like.

'It's a pelican, Richard,' confirmed Sir Francis. 'Now, read off the numbers, my friend.'

'Um… 1641 above the hen, and… 1626 above the pelican.'

'Excellent!' said Sir Francis. 'The difference between 1641 and 1626 is 15. So, we must multiply 3407 by 15 to solve the code and work out the date.'

Sir Francis became very still then, apart from his head, which seemed almost to vibrate as his extraordinary brain went to work. Within twenty seconds, he had the answer: 3407 multiplied by 15 is fifty one thousand, one hundred and five.

'That doesn't sound like a date,' said Richard. 'How are we supposed to work out from that when…' And then he stopped. 'Wait a minute.' He slapped his forehead. 'Of course! It *is* a date…'

'How so?' said the clearly baffled Sir Francis.

'When you write the answer out in numbers, it's 51105.'

He cast around for something to write with and found a sharp pebble. He then wrote 51105 on a patch of muddy ground, putting in some gaps between the numbers, so it looked like this:

5 11 05

'The fifth of November 1605,' said Sir Francis. 'Brilliant!'

As Richard thought more deeply about this date and what it signified, his excitement faded and he went very cold inside. 'The fifth of November is tomorrow, is it not?' he said.

Sir Francis's smile vanished in the same instant. 'Aye, it is,' he said quietly. 'And now everything is falling into place. I see what their plan is, and it is much, much more appalling than I imagined. Tomorrow is the State Opening of Parliament. The king and all his ministers will gather in the House of Lords. Lord Monteagle would have been among them. That's why Tresham sent him the warning letter. The plotters must have placed their gunpowder close to the chamber with the aim of blowing up Parliament.'

'We have to leave for London now!' said Richard.

'It's too late,' sighed Sir Francis. 'The State Opening is in less than 24 hours. We'll never make it in time.'

'No, you most certainly will not!' announced a voice behind them.

They both turned to see Francis Tresham smiling at them from atop a horse. Flanking him were two of his friends, also on horseback. Each of them carried a pistol aimed at the heads of Richard and Sir Francis.

Chapter 20

A Choice of Deaths

WHITEWEBBS, 1ST NOVEMBER 1605

Alice backed away down the corridor as Catesby advanced towards her. All the old fears of this man – fears she thought she'd consigned to her past – came flooding back. She remembered the dark, unsmiling pleasure in his face at her cries of pain, and how he kept saying to the guard: *More! … Again! … Beat her harder!* But now she feared him less as a torturer, and more as her unmasker.

'What are *you* doing here?' Catesby demanded as he waved his pistol at her.

Alice wanted to deny she knew him, but her tongue had become as heavy as a stone in her mouth and she found herself unable to speak. He was about to give away her identity, and she could do nothing about it.

'Alice Fletcher,' he growled. 'That's your name, isn't it?'

'Nay, sir, you are wrong…' cried Alice, suddenly finding her voice.

'You mean Adam, surely,' said Anne. 'This young man is a player with the King's Men. Perhaps you've mistaken him for someone else.'

Catesby laughed. He snagged one of the meat pies from Anne's tray with his hook and munched on it greedily. 'Lady, if you think that, it is you who are mistaken,' he smirked, wiping pastry crumbs from his face with his sleeve. 'You have been duped by an imposter, for this is no player and no boy either. This is Alice Fletcher, a spy in the service of Lord Cecil.'

At first Anne looked confused, until, like a thin beam of sunlight piercing a cloud, her eyes began to sparkle. 'I mistook you for a girl when we first met, and I was right, was I not?' Then the confusion returned: 'But what of the rest of it? You cannot really be a spy. Tell me that part isn't true.'

'N-No – I mean…' It was no good – Alice had to tell her the truth. If she expected honesty from Anne, it was the least she could do. 'I mean *yes*, it's true, I am a spy'. As she said it, she felt hope splinter and crumble – hope that she and this lady, who might very well be her mother, could one day be reconciled. For this deeply devout Catholic woman must now regard Alice as the devil incarnate.

'A spy? For Lord Cecil?' Anne looked horrified, sickened.

'You were never my target,' protested Alice. 'I was watching these people, who are plotting violence against the state…'

'All the time you were using me,' said Anne, now close to tears. 'First you wanted my expertise to help decipher the meaning of that symbol. Then you tried to gain my friendship and trust by… by lying to me… claiming to know my…' She glanced at Father Henry and her hands began to tremble. The tray she was carrying fell with a loud clatter and the meat pies went rolling across the floor.

Anne tried to get her breathing under control. She pressed at her head with both hands as if trying to stem the rise of a headache. Meeting Alice's eyes, she spat: 'You horrid, deceitful girl. I hope I never see you again.' Then she hurried away from them up the corridor and out of sight. Father Henry cast a furious look at Alice before hurrying after Anne. Alice barely noticed, as tears began to flow.

Meanwhile, Catesby, having demolished his first pie, plucked a fallen one from the floor with his hook and began chomping on it. Exposing the unsightly contents of his mouth, he said: 'Like all good medicine, the truth hurts. She needed to be told what you are, which is nothing but a loathsome, maggot-hearted Protestant foot-licker. But your scheming has come far too late, my girl, for the revolution is upon us. In a matter of days, the king and all his lords will be dead.'

With Anne's final, bitter judgement still ringing in her ears, Alice heard little of what Catesby said, until the last part: *In a matter of days, the king and all his lords will be dead…* This made her look up.

'You can't do that,' she said weakly. 'I'll stop you.'

'Try it, you flap-mouthed harpy,' said Catesby jovially. 'You may have thwarted me in 1603, but this time, as I said, you're too late. The plans are set. The die is cast. Besides, I have a different set of plans for you.'

'What do you mean?' she gasped.

'Destroying the old regime is the easy part. The harder task will be to establish a new, Catholic monarchy that's acceptable to all, and that's where you come in.'

'I'd sooner die than help you,' said Alice.

'Oh, you'll die alright. That part's already been decided. The only question is how. Do you want a swift end from the executioner's axe, or something slower and more painful, befitting a hell-bound heretic like yourself – I'm thinking here of a burning at the stake? It's your choice. Help me, and I promise you the axe from a decent headsman who I know can guarantee a clean strike. Refuse me and I'm afraid you're kindling.'

Alice shuddered at the horrid choice facing her.

'What do you want me to do?' she finally asked.

Catesby nodded, satisfied. 'That's the attitude I was hoping for... First of all, you're going to come with us to Coombe Abbey near Coventry. We're taking Anne Vaux and Father Henry, too.'

'What's at Coombe Abbey?'

'Princess Elizabeth, the king's nine-year-old daughter. We're going to seize her, force her to become a Catholic, then place her on the English throne. She'll be a puppet of course, and she'll appoint me as her chief minister.'

'So you're going to rule England.'

'Aye – in effect,' said Catesby.

'And what's my role?'

Catesby screwed up his face. 'By all accounts, the princess is a gleeking, griping, giddy-eyed flap-dragon, not fit to appear in public. She'll undermine us, resist us, and most likely say and do all the wrong things at the official ceremonies she'll be expected to attend. We need someone reliable to stand in for her until we can be sure the new queen is capable of carrying out her assigned role.'

'I can't impersonate a nine-year-old!'

'The public have only the vaguest idea of her age, so have no fear about that. All you need do is look dignified and regal in a coronet and a fancy dress. With your play-acting experience, I've no doubt you can carry it off. Do a good job, and you'll die quick, my little princess – that much I can promise.'

Chapter 21

Remember This Day

WESTMINSTER, 5TH NOVEMBER 1605

uido Fawkes placed a hand on Tom's shoulder. 'Imagine it,' he breathed. 'The king and all his lords, blown to ashes in a mighty explosion. They will perish in the Parliament House, the very birthplace of their evil laws. That is God's will. As it says in the Book of Revelation, "… fire came down from God out of heaven, and devoured them".' Tom felt the grip on his shoulder tighten as Guido's excitement swelled. 'We are God's agents, Claudio, doing His work. The shockwaves from this great blow will spread outwards

from London, through every village and shire. And when the people of England learn that God in His wrath has destroyed His enemies in a righteous fire, they will know it is time to return to the True Faith.'

In the glow of the lantern, Guido's eyes swam with an unearthly light. He was dreaming. But in his dreams, he didn't see the suffering of his victims, the terrible scars and lost limbs. He didn't see the tears of those left to mourn lost loved ones. He saw only righteous fire and God's revenge. In Guido's vision of the future, the English would be so awed by this "great blow" that they would, as one, abandon their religion and eagerly return to the Catholic Church.

But if Tom knew anything about the English, he was sure they would do nothing of the sort. They would view the "great blow" with horror – not as an act of God, but the act of a monster. They would *hate* the man who did this. They'd want to put *him* on a fire and watch him burn. And they'd probably do it every year on the fifth of November just to remind themselves how much they hated him. This gunpowder plot could *not* succeed in its aim of turning England Catholic. Yet it would create an unholy mess. With the monarch and so many lords killed, the kingdom would be left leaderless. There would be civil war, maybe foreign invasion. He had to prevent it.

Guido consulted his pocket watch. 'It is now almost seven in the morning. The king and his lords will assemble above us in two hours' time. We shall watch over the gunpowder together until then.' He shook his bag. 'I have with me sulphur matches and a slow-burning fuse. We'll light the fuse a little before nine o'clock. It will burn for fifteen minutes, giving us time to return to the river and escape in our boat before the gunpowder detonates.'

Tom had to warn Lord Cecil. Yet how could he? There were just two hours before the explosion, and Guido wasn't letting him out of his sight.

'What are your thoughts, Claudio?' Guido asked him. 'You've been very quiet since we've come down here.'

Forcing a smile, Tom stammered a reply: 'I am... amazed. You have done all this, Mr Fawkes. You must have worked on this scheme for many months... I had no idea, when I offered to serve you, what you were preparing and that it would fall to me to play a part in this great, historic... endeavour to rescue England from its, uh... heretical king.'

Guido appeared delighted with this speech. He clapped Tom on the back. 'I'm glad to have you here, Claudio. You opened my eyes to Keyes' treachery, and for that you fully deserve to play your part. It will be your honour, when the time comes, to light the fuse.'

'Gr-Gramercy, Mr Fawkes.'

Tom felt sick. He had to get away, and soon.

'Come, let's sit,' said Guido, setting down his lantern and seating himself on one of a pair of wooden stools. 'We have a little while to go yet.'

'Mr Fawkes, do you mind if I, uh, find a place to relieve myself.'

'There's a privy further along the corridor,' said Guido.

As Tom began walking away, he tried to calculate how long he had. He would have to find his way out of here, run to Whitehall Palace, talk his way past the guards, find Cecil and tell him what was about to happen. By then it could be past eight o'clock. The king might already be entering Parliament, and Guido, realising Tom had betrayed him, would probably detonate the gunpowder early.

Clearly there was not enough time to alert Cecil. He would have to deal with this himself. Perhaps he could overpower Guido. But how? The man was a swordfighting genius, and Tom had no sword.

As he made his way blindly from pillar to pillar in the darkness, his foot accidentally kicked something. He went down on his knees and groped around for it. His fingers closed on a piece of wood – one of the billets. Guido must have dropped it when he was carrying them in here. Tom hefted it in his hand – it felt pleasingly heavy and solid, and might just do as a weapon in a surprise attack. A blow to the head with this, if delivered with enough force, ought to knock him out. But if it didn't, or he missed – Tom didn't like to think about the consequences.

'Are you alright over there, boy?' Guido called. The lantern, now swinging from his hand, came closer.

'Aye, I'm fine – just tripped on something.'

'Sorry for the want of light, old friend. We can't afford to attract attention.'

Tom waited for Guido to return to his stool. He could hear his own breath coming too fast in his ears. Guido scared him – those reptilian eyes, the brutal way he'd decapitated that chicken, and skewered Keyes. The man was hard and quick and utterly ruthless – a born killer. Tom had never faced an adversary like this.

Slowly, quietly, he made his way back to where Guido was seated.

Guido raised his head and smiled good naturedly. 'Back so soon?'

Tom thought he could sense the tiniest hint of puzzlement in Guido's voice, and maybe a spark of unease in his eye – the first inkling that something wasn't right. He had to act now, before that inkling hardened into suspicion. He raised his arm and brought the billet down hard, as hard as he could, on Guido's head.

But something happened while his arm was descending. Guido, with astonishing reflexes, swayed to one side, and the blow caught him not on the head, but on the neck. He collapsed with a roar to the ground, overturning the lantern. As Tom moved in for a second strike, he half glimpsed fire from the lantern spreading to one of the fagots on the pile.

Guido was on the floor, scrambling into the shadows. Tom dived on top of him, pinning him down with one hand while raising the billet to bash him with the other. But Guido, like a snake, slithered from beneath him and staggered to his feet, one hand clasped to his neck, the other one already drawing his sword. Tom, fearing that the momentum was no longer his, threw himself at Guido, but Guido stepped swiftly aside. At the same time, he shoved Tom in the back, sending him crashing to his knees. Tom rose up at once and spun around – right into the flightpath of a swinging blade.

He stopped, his cheek less than an inch from the point of Guido's sword.

Guido grabbed Tom by the scruff of his tunic and dug the point more firmly into his cheek, just below his right eye. Tom barely felt the pain. His head was filled with the smell of smoke, the crackling of flames.

'Claudio, Claudio,' sighed Guido, sounding like a disappointed teacher admonishing a poor pupil. 'I thought you were my friend…'

Any second now, thought Tom, the fire would reach the first barrel, and then *BLAM!* The world would end.

'… The scar on your arm, that story about Father Watson – you had me fooled…'

'Fire,' rasped Tom, eyeballing the spreading flames. 'It's going to go up too early… the king won't die…'

Guido smiled. Grasping Tom more firmly and not once taking his eyes off him, he took a step backwards and kicked the flaming fagot clear of the main pile. Then he stamped on it. Briefly, he looked down to check the fire was out, and as he did so, Tom kicked him hard in the shins. Guido groaned. His grip loosened and Tom broke free and lurched away from him. With the lantern extinguished, the only remaining light came from the embers of the fagot. In its faint pink glow, Tom made out the gleam of the overturned lantern. He picked it up and swung it at Guido, striking him with satisfying force in the middle of the face. Guido staggered backwards into the darkness. Tom advanced slowly, brandishing the lantern, ready to finish him off.

But with every step into the inky void of the undercroft, his confidence diminished and his nerves tightened. *Where was he? Where did he go?*

'I'm right here,' came a nearby whisper.

Tom swished the lantern in the direction of the sound. A hand closed around his flying wrist and his arm was pinned viciously to his back. The lantern was forced out of his hands. Guido then finished off the manoeuvre by fastening an arm around his neck.

'Keyes was right about you,' hissed Guido, his voice now taut with anger. His nose sounded blocked – Tom wondered if he'd broken it. Guido began admonishing himself: 'Keyes tried to warn me, but I wouldn't listen. I liked you too much. I wanted to believe you were loyal. Let my heart rule my head. That'll never happen again.'

He shoved Tom against a pillar, pulling his arms behind him so his back was rammed hard against the pillar's surface. Tom felt the burn of rope on his wrists. Guido was tying him up, trapping him here. Another length of rope was pulled around his waist, securing him more firmly to the pillar. Finally, a dirty cloth was tugged over his mouth and tied painfully tight at the back of his head to gag him. He felt trussed like a Christmas goose, barely able to move, unable to speak. His arms ached from being forced back in this unnatural position.

Guido used the dying ember from the fagot to relight the lantern and then returned to sit on his stool. Tenderly he dabbed at his damaged, bleeding nose. 'We could have made a great team, Claudio,' he said ruefully. 'I had plans to make you my personal servant when all this is over. And I'm going to be a very powerful figure, let me tell you, at the court of Queen Elizabeth II. The power behind the throne will be her chief minister, my good friend Robert Catesby – or Mr Roberts as you know him. I shall be Catesby's right-hand man, and you would have been mine – servant to the second most powerful man in England. How about that? Instead, you're going to die like the miserable spy you are. You're going to die, along with all the other sinners and heretics who will shortly be filling the chamber above us.'

He checked his pocket watch, and sighed. 'Dawn has broken. The start of a new day, and what a day it will be! The fifth of November 1605. People will remember this day, Claudio. They'll celebrate it for centuries to come. My name will go down in history.

Yours could have, too, if you'd chosen to join me. But you chose the path of betrayal, and now your name will be incinerated along with your body. Nothing will be left of you, and no one will remember you.'

Tom struggled against his bonds, but it was no good. The ropes were thick and the knots tight. His little belt knife was well out of reach. He'd run out of options. And in just over an hour, the king and his ministers would start taking their places above them in the House of Lords.

Act Five

Chapter 22

The Dash South

RUSHTON HALL–WESTMINSTER,
4–5TH NOVEMBER 1605

Richard stared in dismay at the mounted trio of Francis Tresham, Thomas Percy and Robert Wintour. Tresham had the jaunty air of an angler who had just caught two prize fish. But his sidekicks wore expressions as cold and severe as their pistols, currently aimed at Richard and Sir Francis.

Tresham glanced up at the Triangular Lodge. 'So you worked out the code. I offer my congratulations! Sadly for you, your clever piece of deduction has come too late. We're leaving today – all of us, including you two. We're heading to Coombe Abbey in Warwickshire where we plan to meet up with the leader of our little enterprise, Robert Catesby.' Keeping his gaze fastened upon Richard and Sir Francis, he said to his companions: 'Bring them in.'

As Percy and Wintour trotted forwards, pistols raised, Richard made a desperate decision. He could not afford to be recaptured – it would mean the death of any hope of stopping this plot. He could make a dash for the forest now – it was but twenty yards from where he stood, and with luck he might not get shot as he ran. Once under tree cover, he would be in his natural element, and his chances of survival would be greatly increased. The problem was that while he could reach the forest in a matter of seconds by himself, this would mean leaving Sir Francis at the mercy of Tresham. It was not in Richard's nature to abandon his friends. Yet when weighed against his duty to protect the king from mortal peril, what other choice did he have? He thought – *hoped!* – Sir Francis would agree.

All this flashed through Richard's mind, though perhaps not in so logical a form, in less than a second, and before he quite knew himself that the decision had been made, he turned and began his dash for the trees. He ran not in a straight line, but in a darting manner, first one way, then the other, trying to make himself as hard a target as possible for the gunmen.

A shot split the air, and a clump of mud and grass a few feet to his left exploded. Another bang, and he felt the bullet's scorching breath inches from his right ear. A horse whinnied and hoofbeats drummed the earth. Richard charged on, fear driving him faster. He raced past the first, sparse trees of the forest before plunging into its dense interior, feeling its green-tinged shade like the embrace of an old friend.

Behind him, the horsemen kept coming. The rumble of hooves shook the forest floor, and branches snapped as they crashed through the trees. Richard decided on a change of tactics. Instead of continuing in a forward direction as his pursuers might expect, he went upwards. Finding a large beech tree with a vertical split in its trunk, he clawed his way up through the middle of it and, with the nimbleness of a squirrel, darted swiftly along one of its branches.

There he crouched, some fifteen feet above the ground, listening. He could hear Percy and Wintour moving more hesitantly now as they navigated what paths they could find between the trees. Wintour soon emerged into view. As he trotted beneath the beech tree, Richard dropped from his perch onto the horse's hindquarters. The shock and momentum of this sudden ambush was enough to knock Wintour to the ground. The startled horse neighed and tried to bolt, but Richard managed to grab the reins and hold on. After manoeuvring himself into the vacated saddle, he brought the horse under control. Now he had some transport!

He rode deeper into the forest in what he believed to be a south-westerly direction, his horse stumbling several times on exposed roots. At length, he chanced upon a bridleway and was able to spur the horse to greater speed. He could no longer hear any sounds of pursuit. Percy, he assumed, had given up. Already, Richard's prospects were looking brighter. The next step was to find the road to Westminster. The time, according to the position of the sun, he reckoned to be mid-morning – that meant he had less than twenty-four hours to cover eighty miles, if he was to save the king. It was a mighty challenge, considering it had taken he and Sir Francis a full forty-eight hours to do the same journey from London by coach.

Upon reaching a main road, he followed a sign to the village of Kettering. He rode hard, goading his horse to its maximum speed, and reached Wellingborough by midday. By five o'clock, the horse was frothing at the mouth and utterly exhausted. At an inn outside Bedford he picked up a fresh mount, and bought himself a loaf of bread, a hunk of cheese and an apple. Then he continued his journey, chewing as he galloped through the gathering dark. Even a short rest was out of the question – to stand the faintest chance of reaching Westminster in time for the State Opening, he would have to ride through the night.

Richard flew into Luton at one o'clock in the morning. Three hours later, he reached St Albans. By now, his head was drooping close to the pommel of his saddle, and he was in frequent danger of falling from his horse. The tired animal, sensing his rider's sluggishness, slowed to a canter. Richard was conscious he had just five hours to traverse the final twenty miles. He roused the ostler at an inn near Radlett and paid him the last of his money for the fastest horse in his stable. Wearily, he mounted it, and rode with all the energy he could muster along the arrow-straight Roman road of Watling Street. The villages flashed by in a blur: Borehamwood, Edgware, Hendon. At dawn, he passed through the hamlet of Kentish Town, and the church of St Martin-in-the-Fields was striking eight o'clock by the time he approached Charing Cross.

Here, Richard's progress began to be hindered by increasing amounts of foot traffic as people converged on Westminster, hoping for a sight of their monarch. King James had begun his journey early that morning, travelling up the river by barge from his residence at Greenwich Palace for a service at Westminster Abbey. The service, Richard guessed had now ended, and the king would be on his way to the House of Lords for the State Opening of Parliament.

To have any chance of stopping the royal progress, Richard had to find Lord Cecil and tell him about the plot. If he tried explaining the situation to anyone else, they would dismiss his tale as the ravings of a madman. The trouble was he had no idea where Cecil was. He shouted at the throngs of dawdling citizenry filling the street in front of him, imploring them to make way for him. Most just ignored him; some swore at him or made rude gestures. Eventually, he was obliged to abandon his horse and continue on foot. It was easier to advance this way, as he could weave through the crowds, and dart along narrow alleys.

Finally, Richard reached Old Palace Yard, the great open public space that lay between Westminster Abbey and the Palace of Westminster. The Palace wasn't a single structure but a cluster of grand old buildings huddled around the enormous edifice of Westminster Hall. One of these buildings was the House of Lords. Enormous crowds lined the way between the Abbey and the Lords. Richard could hear them cheering and saw caps being flung in the air. He assumed this meant the king was now in public view, making his way on foot between the two buildings. He hurried forward, fighting his way through streams of labourers, shopkeepers, craftsmen, apprentices, tourists, merchants and beggars. Many cursed, thumped and kicked him as he pushed past them, but Richard didn't care. All that mattered was that the king did not complete his walk and enter the Lords.

It took time – time Richard could ill afford – but eventually he managed to squeeze his way to the front of the crowd. A cordon of guards armed with long, sharp halberds held the onlookers back, and peering over their well-muscled shoulders Richard was able to catch his first glimpse of the king. James was proceeding slowly towards some steps that led to the Lords' arched entrance. Now and then, he would turn and wave at his subjects, prompting a huge cheer. The king was wearing a long, crimson robe of state and was accompanied by a retinue of beautifully attired and coiffured courtiers. To his left walked a peer bearing the Cap of Maintenance, a crimson velvet hat lined with ermine, and to his right strode another carrying the Sword of State. Behind him came the Lord Chamberlain bearing his white wand of office. He was followed by the bishops and the lords temporal – dukes, earls and judges. And behind them came the members of the House of Commons with the Speaker, dressed in black and gold, in their midst.

It was a stirring sight – the entire ruling elite of England all gathering here for this ancient ceremony. It was also, for Richard, a terrifying one, as he watched these people heading for their probable doom. Once inside that chamber, their lives might be numbered in minutes. He wanted to yell a warning, but they were too far away, and his voice would be one of thousands, lost in the general din. Instead, he shouted at the guard nearest to him in the cordon: 'You have to let me through! I have urgent news for Lord Cecil!'

The guard's serious face broke into a snigger. 'Sure you have, son. And my uncle's the King of Morocco!'

'It's true!' cried Richard. 'The king's life is in danger if he goes into that building. There is a plot...'

The guard scowled, no longer finding anything

amusing in the exchange. 'Go to, you prating fool!' he said, shoving Richard backwards with the shaft of his halberd.

Richard could only look on in despair as the doors of the House of Lords opened and the king and his retinue began to enter.

Chapter 23

Fifteen Minutes

WESTMINSTER, 5TH NOVEMBER 1605

uido Fawkes cocked an ear towards the ceiling of the undercroft. 'Hear that, Claudio? They're coming in.'

Tom could hear it – the muffled creak of footsteps high above them, and he pictured the king and his courtiers filling up the chamber.

'It's time,' said Guido, rising from his stool and stretching his limbs.

Tom wished he could also move. He wrestled once again with his bonds, but it was a hopeless gesture, born of despair. The knots were too tight. His arms, his mouth, everything ached. His gag was soaked with sour-tasting spit.

He could only watch as Guido ignited one of his sulphur matches in the lantern, then carried the precarious flame to the far end of the five-yard-long twine fuse that snaked across the floor. As Guido crouched down to touch the flame to the fuse, it sparked and smouldered. And the glowing, fiery tip began its slow, deliberate journey towards the great pile of gunpowder barrels and fuel heaped against the rear wall of the undercroft.

Satisfied that the fuse was successfully lit, Guido started towards the exit. Then he stopped and turned to Tom. 'I'm leaving now, Claudio,' he told him. 'You have fifteen minutes to reflect on your life and the choices you have made. It is a pity you won't live to see the world you failed to prevent: Catholic England reborn, rising like the Phoenix from the ashes of this evil house.'

'You'll burn in Hell for this, Guy Fawkes!' yelled Tom, deliberately calling him by his despised, English name. At least that was what he tried to say, but the gag on his mouth turned his words to gibberish.

Guido chuckled to himself as he hastened from the undercroft. 'Fare thee well, my friend. Have a pleasant death…' Tom could hear echoing laughter from the stairwell as Guido made his way up the steps that would take him out of the building.

Silence fell – or *near* silence. From high above, Tom could hear the soft shuffle of people moving about, the faint scrape of chairs, the muted rumble of voices. Closer at hand, he could hear the crackle of smouldering twine as the flame steadily burned its way through the fuse. Already it seemed several feet closer to its destination. Guido had left behind the lantern. It lit up the base of the mound of fuel-covered gunpowder and Tom could see exactly where the fuse entered the pile. Maybe Guido had done this deliberately, so Tom would be able to witness the flame hitting the gunpowder, and hence know the precise second of his death.

Was this a small act of kindness on Guido's part – or the opposite? It was hard to be sure. Had he ever liked Tom, or had it all been an act? He'd seemed genuinely shocked and upset when Tom turned on him. And Tom had to admit he'd enjoyed the man's company; for a while at least, a mutual respect had existed between them – until Guido had let the charming mask slip, exposing the cold-eyed religious fanatic beneath.

The flame was now just ten feet or so from the gunpowder. It was burning through the fuse quickly, at a rate of about a foot a minute, Tom estimated, giving him just ten more minutes.

He tugged and heaved with all his might at the rope binding his waist and wrists. He strained his muscles until they screamed their distress. The knots failed to yield even slightly – if anything they grew tighter each time he pulled at them. Since he couldn't move, all he had left was his voice. He began to scream as loudly as he could through the spit-drenched gag, praying that someone, somewhere, might hear him.

He yelled and shouted until he was hoarse and his cries rebounded off the heartless stone walls and faded to silence.

No one was coming. He'd failed. The king and all his lords would die. England was doomed. It was the end of Tom Cavendish, too, and in these final moments, thoughts of his country receded as the span of his awareness dwindled to himself and those he loved.

…Reflect on your life and the choices that you made…

That was what Guido had advised. Yet when he tried to, all Tom felt was a burning regret at all the experiences he would never have, and the people he would never see again. Never again would he assist his brilliant master Sir Francis Bacon in his laboratory, helping him shine lanterns on the dark corners of the universe. Only a few weeks ago, they had talked of embarking on a new project – exploring *electricus*, the strange attractive force described by William Gilbert, which Sir Francis was convinced could one day be harnessed as a form of energy.

Glancing up, he saw there were just five feet of fuse left.

He would never learn about *electricus*…

And Alice. Tom would miss her more than anyone. How sad that he never got to solve the mystery of what he loved about her, or who the real Alice even was. Did he love the sweet and tragic Ophelia, the part she'd been playing when he first set eyes on her? Alice was sure he'd never completely managed to separate her from that role. Perhaps she was right. But he also loved the adventurous, funny, fun-loving Alice of real life – though even that sometimes seemed to him like an act. He'd glimpse her at odd moments, when she thought no one was looking, close to tears – maybe thinking about her childhood – and he wondered if she wasn't closer to Hamlet's girlfriend than she cared to admit. Either way, whether Alice or Ophelia, he wanted to be with her, to share in her happiness and comfort her when she was sad. He didn't want to imagine Alice growing up, or growing old, without him.

Thoughts of Alice. Thoughts of the life they could have had. And all the while, the seconds ticked by and the flame burned ever closer to the powder…

Chapter 24

Race Against Time

WESTMINSTER, 5TH NOVEMBER 1605

Among the peers filing into the House of Lords, Richard spied one who was much shorter than the rest. He had a long face, made even longer by his pointed beard and swept back hair.

Lord Cecil!

'There he is!' cried Richard, jumping up and down to make himself more visible to those beyond the cordon of guards. 'It's Lord Cecil! Let me through. I need to speak with him!'

'Get back I tell you, or do you want to feel the point of this?' said the now exasperated guard, aiming his halberd at Richard.

But Richard had also lost patience. He hadn't ridden eighty miles and gone twenty-four hours without sleep to be thwarted at the last moment – not with Lord Cecil within sight. He pushed the halberd aside, dropped to his knees and squirmed and slithered between the guard's legs. The enraged guard tried to beat him with the shank of his weapon, but Richard was too quick and too determined, and he was soon through the the guard's legs and beyond the cordon. Scrambling to his feet he began sprinting towards the line of ministers passing through the entrance, crying 'Lord Cecil! Lord Cecil! It's me, Richard Fletcher!'

But Cecil had, by this time, already entered the chamber. Richard continued nevertheless to race towards the Lords. Behind him he could hear the pounding footsteps and shouts of guards in pursuit. They yelled to their comrades protecting the dignitaries in the queue, and half a dozen of these now began charging at Richard from the steps of the Lords. Seeing he was about to be pincered between these two lines of converging guards, Richard veered east and ran down a narrow, gloomy side street on the southern side of the building. Before the guards caught sight of him, he skidded left into a covered alleyway and took shelter in its shade. Here he waited, gasping for breath, as the pursuing guards thundered by.

Once they were gone, he considered his next move. He was now behind the House of Lords. Perhaps he could find another way in, and try and pass on a warning to Cecil. He walked on to the far end of the covered alley and found himself in a cobbled square. One side of the square was taken up by the rear wall of the House of Lords, but he could find no entryway there. A row of small, single-storey houses took up another side of the square. Richard was about to knock on the door of one of these to ask for help when he was distracted by a sound of approaching footsteps. Was it one of the guards coming back for him? No, this was coming from another direction – from a tiny passage he hadn't noticed before that ran between the row of houses and the north wall of the Lords.

Suddenly, a man dashed out of the passage into the square, lurching to a halt when he saw Richard, and blinking as if he hadn't seen sunlight in a while. The man was tall, with glossy, red-brown hair and the muscular build of a soldier. There were traces of blood around his nose, which looked bruised as if recently broken. He began striding quickly across the square, but Richard stepped in front of him, forcing him to stop. 'Greetings, friend,' Richard exclaimed. 'Prithee, do you know of a back entrance to the Lords?'

The fellow pushed past Richard and walked on a few paces, before stopping abruptly and turning to face him. 'Why do you ask?'

'I have an urgent message for Lord Cecil. I believe the king's life is in danger.'

'Is that so?' said the man, his eyebrows converging in a frown. 'By my troth, that does sound urgent. It so happens there is a back entrance, if you'd care to follow me.'

'Gramercy, sir,' said Richard.

As he began to follow him, Richard thought he heard a faint screaming sound. It seemed to come from underground, but surely that was impossible. It was probably just the squeal of a coach wheel on a nearby street.

'I am surprised I failed to find the entrance myself, for I came this way just now,' Richard remarked as they approached the covered alley.

'It is easy to miss in the dark,' answered the man.

His voice sounded relaxed, but there was something disquieting about his gait – his head low and thrust forward, his limbs loose, ears erect. It reminded Richard of stalking wolves he had encountered during evenings in the forest.

They entered the gloom of the covered alley, and Richard tensed. Where was he being led? There was no back entrance in here.

Suddenly, the man whirled around, fist raised, aimed for Richard's jaw. But Richard, his instincts by now on full alert, was ready. With the reflexes of a forest survivor, he sprang backwards. The weight and momentum of the punch forced the man off-balance.

Before he could recover, Richard socked him hard in the stomach. The man fell to the cobbles, doubled up in pain. Richard leaned down and grabbed him by the collar, pulling him up so their faces were inches apart.

'Who are you?' he growled.

The man, still winded, managed a defiant smile. 'Guido Fawkes,' he gasped.

Guido Fawkes. Where had he heard that name before?

'Why did you just attack me, Mr Fawkes?'

'Attack you, old friend?' said Guido innocently. 'Why, you have it backwards. You attacked *me*. I was merely turning around to tell you *this*.'

Richard felt a sharp kick to the back of his left leg. At the same time his right arm was tugged violently downwards. He lost his footing and a second later found himself lying on his back with Guido's knee pressing down upon his windpipe.

It came to Richard then, as he struggled for breath, where he'd heard the name *Guido Fawkes* before. Sir Francis had mentioned him as one of the conspirators, along with Catesby and Tresham.

'You know where the gunpowder is,' Richard wheezed.

Guido drew a small knife from his belt. 'The fuse is already lit,' he said through a gritted-teeth smile, 'and you have delayed me long enough. I should have been on the river and away by now.'

He aimed the blade at Richard's exposed throat and thrust downwards. At the same time, Richard used all his remaining strength to roll hard to his right. He felt a sharp, glistening line of pain as the blade sliced deep into the skin of his neck. Guido raised his knife for a second attack, but before he could deliver it, he was knocked sideways as Richard rolled the other way and swung a vicious clout to the side of his head.

Richard pushed the dazed Guido off his chest, and leapt to his feet. He clamped a hand to his neck. Warm blood leaked through his fingers. Guido flailed with his knife, cutting Richard's leg. Then Richard kicked out with his other leg, and the knife went clattering across the cobbles. He kicked Guido again, this time much harder and in the head, and Guido groaned and fell still.

Grabbing his collar, Richard shook him and shouted: 'Where's the gunpowder?' Guido's eyes fluttered open. He stared at Richard, who bellowed at him once more: 'Where's the gunpowder?'

Guido continued to stare blankly at him, saying nothing. Richard couldn't tell if his silence was deliberate or not. His eyes appeared empty of all feeling, and perhaps he hadn't even understood the question.

After three more attempts at getting information out of him, Richard gave up. He released Guido and ran back into the cobbled square. He was feeling light-headed, probably from the loss of blood, which now stained his collar and the shoulder of his tunic.

He recalled that Guido had emerged from a narrow passage on the north side of the Lords, and this was where he now ran. There was one entrance, halfway along – a small arched doorway standing ajar. Keeping one hand pressed to his neck, he entered the doorway and walked down a spiral stone stairwell. At the bottom he found a dark, cavernous space – an enormous undercroft the size of the chamber of the House of Lords directly above. Two parallel lines of pillars ran all the way to the far end, where a lantern illuminated an enormous pile of what looked like wood chips.

At that moment, a terrible sound filled his ears. It was like a hoarse, demented screaming – and Richard recognised it as the noise he'd heard much more faintly earlier in the square. It was coming from the far end of the undercroft, near the lantern and the big wood pile. Richard ran towards the screamer, and as he came closer he saw, with a rush of excitement and alarm, that it was Tom, tied to one of the pillars. He rushed up to him and began untying the ropes that bound him. But the ropes became sticky with blood from his fingers, and he struggled with the knots. Meanwhile, Tom only screamed louder. He was trying desperately to speak, but his words were muffled by the gag in his mouth. Richard noticed Tom was staring in pure horror at the wood pile, his eyeballs straining from his head. Richard turned to see what he was staring at, and then very nearly screamed himself.

A flame was flickering near the base of the pile, burning through the final inches of a fuse, and it was starting to lick at a barrel buried inside the wood – Richard recognised it as one of the barrels he'd seen six days ago being loaded onto the back of a cart at the Port of London – the barrels containing gunpowder! He looked again at the enormous pile and realised with a terrifying certainty that the whole towering mass was full of these barrels, and in a matter of seconds they were all going to explode.

He flew towards the pile, reached in and pulled the last red-hot inch of fuse clear of the barrel. It scorched his hand and he dropped it on the floor. But something was still burning in the pile. Extending his arm, he managed to retrieve a bundle of sticks that had caught alight. He threw that down next to the remnant of fuse and stamped on it several times. When they were extinguished, he turned his attention to the barrel. It was smoking and had a charred patch on its staves, but the flame, thank Heaven, hadn't penetrated very deep into its surface. To be safe, however, he heaved the hot barrel out of the pile and carefully carried it across the thirty-yard extent of the undercroft and placed it outside in the stairwell, behind a thick stone wall – if it exploded now, it wouldn't have the power to detonate the rest. From above him, in the street, came sounds of urgent voices and footsteps. He hoped, if it was the guards, that they had found and arrested Guido Fawkes. As for Richard, his priority was now Tom.

He raced back to the far end of the undercroft and hastily untied and ungagged him. When Tom was free, they embraced silently – there were no words to describe what they had just been through, how close they had come to death, or England to cataclysm.

'What happened to your neck?' Tom asked.

'Guido Fawkes did it,' said Richard weakly as another wave of dizziness passed through him.

Above them, the clunking footsteps and shouts had been steadily rising in volume, and suddenly the stairwell resounded with the clatter of heavily shod men. Guards swarmed into the undercroft. In the lead was the one from the cordon whose legs Richard had squeezed through.

'There he is!' he bellowed when he saw Richard. 'I told you he was up to no good! Let's get him!'

'Wait!' cried Richard, as they stormed towards him. 'Look at this!' He gestured at the great pile of sticks and barrels behind him. 'This is what I was trying to prevent!'

The guards shambled to a halt as they came within sight of the mountainous heap. They stared up at it, struggling to comprehend what it was or why it was here.

Then a tiny figure pushed his way through to the ranks of guards to the front. Lord Cecil was in his beautiful crimson-and-black Order of the Garter robes, having come straight from the State Opening ceremony upstairs. With his quick, birdlike eyes, he appraised first Richard and Tom, taking in the deep wound in Richard's neck, and the sword cut below Tom's right eye and the other one in his finger.

Then he turned his attention to the huge wood stack behind them, with the barrels just visible beneath its cloak of kindling.

'Did you boys stop this lot from going up?' he asked.

'Aye,' said Richard.

'Then on behalf of England, I thank you,' he said quietly. 'How did you discover it was here?'

'It is a long story, sire,' said Richard, 'which we will gladly tell you. But right now–'

'You must go after Guido Fawkes!' broke in Tom. 'He did this.'

'I left him wounded and barely conscious beneath a covered alley behind this building,' said Richard.

Cecil gave instructions to some of the guards, who ran off to try and find him.

A few minutes later, they reported back with troubling news: Guido was gone. Cecil immediately organised a street-by-street search of the area. Meanwhile, Tom and Richard were escorted to Whitehall Palace for further questioning. Cecil arranged for his personal physician to treat their wounds.

Chapter 25

The Princess

COOMBE ABBEY, 6ᵀᴴ NOVEMBER 1605

'There's Coombe Abbey,' said Father Henry Garnet, pointing from the window of their coach. They had crested a small hill, and spread beneath them in the tawny-gold dusk was a patchwork of fields and forests. In their midst was a large and handsome house surrounded by formal gardens and straight rows of trees.

'It looks a fitting home for a princess, don't you agree, Mistress,' said Alice.

Anne ignored the question, her expression cold.

She hadn't said a word to Alice all journey.

Catesby, from the front seat of the coach, must have sensed the tension for he turned around and bellowed at Anne: 'Answer her, woman! Remember, she's going to be your queen in a few days' time!'

'Fake queen,' said Anne contemptuously. 'It will be a fitting role for a young woman who has led such a deceitful life.'

Catesby raised his arm to strike Anne, and Father Henry interposed himself in an attempt to protect her, until he was jerked back into his seat by the guard sitting next to him.

Alice said hastily: 'Prithee, sir, stay your hand. I am not offended.'

Catesby cursed under his breath and turned away from them. An unpleasant silence settled over the coach as they swept through the main gates of Coombe Abbey and trundled up the long driveway.

They were greeted at the entrance by Francis Tresham. He and Catesby embraced.

'We have secured the princess,' reported Tresham.

'Excellent! How is she behaving?'

'Badly. She's refusing all food. We're having to force it down her throat.'

Catesby frowned. 'That eel-skinned young plague sore! It is fortunate we have a willing surrogate.' He pointed to Alice, who glared back at him through the coach window, hating the compliant role he was forcing upon her.

'Adam?' exclaimed Tresham. 'You want a boy to play a queen?'

'Not Adam – Alice,' said Catesby. 'She fooled you and many others about her gender, and she'll fool the country that she's their monarch.'

Tresham studied Alice more intensely. 'The devious little witch. I had no idea…'

'Any word from London?' asked Catesby.

'None yet,' said Tresham. 'But I expect news at any hour of our mission's success.'

'Guy won't let us down,' said Catesby. 'He planned everything to the last detail, and recruited an able and willing young assistant to boot. Thirty-six barrels of gunpowder – enough to rip the heart out of Protestant England. The king and all his ministers must have been blown to ashes.'

Hearing these words pushed Alice into a state of cold fear and anger. She pictured smoke drifting upwards from the blackened shell of the Parliament House, the unidentifiable remains of the king, his lords, bishops and who knew how many commoners, amid the embers. *How dare they!* She thought of Tom and Richard, both of whom might have been there at the scene, and she felt sick.

Father Henry clutched Anne's hand. 'Nothing good can come of this,' he said, as Anne began to weep.

Tresham had tears in his eyes, too, but for very different reasons. 'The world we have for so long yearned for is now upon us,' he said, as he embraced

Catesby once more. 'England is in our hands. It is time for us to act…'

The sound of approaching hoofbeats on gravel alerted everyone to a new arrival.

'It's Guido!' cried Tresham, breaking free of Catesby in order to greet the mounted figure galloping down the drive towards them.

Alice assumed Guido must be Guy. She craned her neck out of the window to behold the mass murderer. Her first thought was that he looked somewhat broken. He was not erect in his saddle, but leaning heavily to one side, his head drooping and bouncing against his chest as if he was only half conscious.

Guido drew up sharply in front of Tresham and Catesby and would have toppled to the ground had Tresham not caught him and helped him down.

His clothing bore the filth of the road. 'Water!' he rasped through a slack dry mouth. Catesby unscrewed his flask and handed it to him. Everyone watched Guido glug it down. They took in the smashed nose, the dark bruise on his neck, and Alice saw alarm brightening the eyes of Tresham and Catesby.

Tresham was biting hard on his lower lip. 'Tell us, Guido,' he urged, once the man had drunk his fill. 'What news?'

Guido's face seemed to shrivel as he said: 'I have failed you, gentlemen.'

'No!' wailed Tresham, collapsing to his knees. Inside the coach, Alice silently cheered, while Anne and Father

Henry raised their eyes in thanks to Heaven.

Catesby grabbed Guido by his filthy collar and placed his hook menacingly close to the man's eye. 'What do you mean, failed me?' he roared.

'First I was betrayed by my assistant. But I managed to deal with him. Then another young man confronted me as I was leaving the undercroft. He must have learned of our plans somehow, for he hoped to warn the king that his life was in danger. I tried to kill him, but he survived my attack and beat me half unconscious.'

Alice squeezed her fists tight in her excitement. She was sure the young man in question was either Richard or Tom.

'When I came to, I witnessed scores of royal guards pouring into the undercroft. I suppose the young man led them there. They must have found the gunpowder and extinguished the fuse. I beg your forgiveness Mr Catesby. Someone has betrayed us, or how did this youth learn of our plans?'

Catesby dropped Guido to the ground and turned on Tresham. 'Francis,' he said in a dangerously low voice, 'has your big mouth been flapping again?'

'By my faith, of course not!' protested Tresham, rising to his feet and backing away from Catesby.

'Only we three knew the timing and location of the explosion,' said Catesby. 'I didn't tell anyone. Neither, I am sure, did Guido. So that leaves you… Did you, by any chance, write to that foolborn brother-in-law of yours?'

Francis gasped. 'I–I only wanted to warn Lord Monteagle not to go to Parliament that day, but I wrote the letter in a code that only he would understand, and he would never have told anyone…'

'Traitor!' screamed Catesby, and he struck Tresham hard across the face with the side of his hook.

Tresham fell to the ground, clutching his bloodied cheek and weeping. It was hard to know if his tears were prompted by pain, guilt or sorrow, but it may have been all three.

'We cannot remain here,' Guido said. 'The Sheriff of Worcester is on our tail with hundreds of men.'

'Then we shall go to our hideout at Holbeche House in Staffordshire,' said Catesby. 'We have gunpowder and weapons stored there and we can make a final stand.'

'But Holbeche is more than thirty miles from here,' objected Tresham. 'We'll never make it.'

Catesby made to strike him once again. Tresham flinched and said no more. Addressing Guido, Catesby said: 'If we leave now, we can ride through the night and be there by morning. We still have the princess – she is now our most prized asset. It will force the king to negotiate with us.'

'What about the King's Men?' asked Tresham nervously.

'We'll leave them here,' said Catesby. 'They might have proved useful had everything gone to plan. With the king dead, we could have deployed them to start the process of winning over the populace. Unfortunately, some maggot-brained fool blew all such hopes apart with a letter. I'd advise that man to say nothing more if he wishes to keep his tongue in his head.'

In less than an hour, they were back on the road, and this time the party travelled in two coaches. Father Henry and Mistress Anne were placed in the front coach, while Alice was seated in the rear one with a new travelling companion – Princess Elizabeth. Alice had expected to feel some sympathy for the young prisoner, but she quickly grew to hate her. Sympathy, if anything, was due to her poor guards, whose arms and faces were covered in scratches and bite marks delivered by the royal fingernails and teeth.

'I want to go home,' demanded Elizabeth, a long-nosed girl with a pointy chin and curly raven hair. 'If you don't take me back home this very minute my father will kill you. He'll hang you, and when you're nearly dead he'll chop you down and cut you open and burn your guts in front of you. Then he'll tie your limbs to four strong horses and we'll all cheer as you are torn apart. Then he'll put your heads on spikes on London Bridge so everyone can see what happens to traitors. That's what he'll do.'

A spirited girl, one might say – even a brave one? Alice didn't think so, for when the guards ignored her threats, the princess burst into tears and stamped her slippered foot. And when that didn't work, she went back to scratching and biting them. The guards restrained her and defended themselves as best they could, although this was difficult, as Tresham had strictly forbidden them from leaving any bruising on the royal skin. When one of the guards pulled her hand a little too roughly from his eyes, Elizabeth screeched: 'He hurt me! The big fat pig hurt my arm!'

Tresham, who was seated up front, turned around and warned the guard: 'Watch yourself if you value your life!'

The guard gritted his teeth, and the girl's eyes twinkled with malicious delight. She whispered to Alice: 'Why don't you steal his dagger and stick it in him? He dare not fight us back.'

Alice, alarmed, shook her head.

'Will you not act to protect the king's own daughter?' Elizabeth challenged her. When Alice didn't respond, disappointment soon turned to contempt: 'Just as I thought, you have no spine.'

Chapter 26

The Locket

HOLBECHE HOUSE, 7ᵀᴴ NOVEMBER 1605

Alice was relieved when dawn broke and they pulled into the forecourt of Holbeche House. Eager to stretch her limbs and make her escape from the princess from hell, Alice was first out of the coach. Princess Elizabeth was helped out next, and was escorted, cursing and struggling all the way, to an upper-storey room of the house.

Meanwhile, other guards led Alice, Anne and Father Henry along a corridor towards the rear of the house. They passed through an armoury containing arquebuses, calivers, muskets, pistols and several barrels of gunpowder. Beyond this room lay a bare, stone-walled chamber with a single window, which became their cell.

With no chairs available, the three of them sat on the floor, Anne and Henry next to each other, with Alice maintaining a polite distance. The awkward atmosphere that had accompanied the journey to Coombe Abbey now settled upon them once again, with Anne pointedly refusing even to look at Alice or acknowledge her existence. After a prolonged and tortuous silence, Father Henry rose to his feet and began pacing the room. Two or three times he jumped up to try and see out of the small, barred window high up on the back wall, which would have afforded a view of the grounds to the rear of the house. But his efforts were to no avail – the window was too high.

He resumed his pacing. 'Alice is here as a surrogate queen – but what is to become of us?' he wondered aloud.

'We shall be killed, most probably,' said Anne.

'If they wanted to kill us, they could have done so at Coombe Abbey,' said Henry. 'Why did they bother bringing us all this way? And it can't simply be to provide them with hostages. Will Shakespeare would have been of far greater value as a hostage than either of us.'

'They have the king's daughter,' said Anne. 'No one has greater hostage value than her – not even Shakespeare. As for you and I, Henry, I have no idea why they brought us here. Perhaps they were in such a panic to leave Coombe Abbey, they weren't thinking straight.'

'But don't you see your own value, Mistress?' said Alice. 'You have connections with the entire recusant community. You are known and respected by all of them. The conspirators need you if they're to have any chance of winning over moderate English Catholics to their cause. As for you, Father, you are the leader of the Jesuits here in England. Catesby and his friends will want you to give the Church's official blessing to their scheme.'

'That will never happen,' Henry answered firmly. 'In any case I am not a papal legate and I have no power to bless anything in the Church's name... But you may be right, young lady. That may indeed be their thinking, however misguided.'

'If that is their thinking,' said Anne, 'then we should prepare for death, for neither of us will ever endorse this evil plot.'

'Of course you won't, Mistress,' agreed Alice. 'It goes against everything you believe in. Even so, I beseech you not to give up on life so soon. While we still have breath, there is hope. The Sheriff of Worcester may get here before they can kill us.'

Anne looked at Alice for perhaps the first time since she had stormed away from her at Whitewebbs. Her expression was fierce, or attempted to be so. *She is determined to think the worst of me*, thought Alice, *but she isn't finding it so easy any more.*

'Henry,' said Anne, 'please inform the girl that I appreciate her kind remarks.'

'I believe she heard you herself,' smiled Henry. 'Now, if you will excuse me, ladies, I would like to pray.' Facing the rear wall, he went down on his knees, put his hands together, and began murmuring a Latin invocation.

Alice continued sitting there next to Anne, and for the first time since they left Whitewebbs, the silence between them felt bearable. The ice-wall of hatred that Anne had erected seemed to have melted a little.

Then Alice noticed that Anne was crying.

'What is it, Mistress?'

'If I die today,' Anne sobbed quietly, 'then it will be as if my children never lived. For I am the only one who knows of their existence and their kinship to me. It breaks my heart that when I die, the memory of two more will die with me, and their passing will never be mourned.'

'Then tell Father Henry about them,' whispered Alice.

Anne shook her head. 'I cannot.'

'Then tell me.'

'You?' Flames of anger flared beneath the sorrow. 'But you are a Protestant spy wh-who came into my house, who befriended me, to get information…'

'I confess,' said Alice, 'that when I first questioned you about that symbol, it was to obtain information about Tresham. But later, when you told me about your children, my curiosity and sympathy were entirely unfeigned, and remain so. For I swear to you I was a child at Christ's Hospital around the time you left your children there.'

Anne looked deeply into Alice's eyes then, and Alice felt her searching them for evidence of honesty. Eventually, Anne said: 'If what you say is true, then perhaps you can do as you promised earlier and tell me if you remember them.'

Alice felt a familiar cool weight against her chest – the locket. It had been Richard's originally, but for near five years now, she had been wearing it. She first put it on in early 1601, when Richard disappeared, as a memento of her lost brother. When he returned more than two years later, he didn't ask for it back, and she didn't offer it – she wasn't sure why. Its original significance, after all, was hateful to her.

A priest at the orphanage had presented the locket to Richard on his tenth birthday. The priest told him it had been left with them by their mother on the steps of the orphanage. Inside the locket was a picture of a woman. Alice hadn't looked at the picture in the locket for many years, yet she hadn't forgotten the face in there. And when, upon her arrival at Whitewebbs, she first saw Anne, her face was familiar – and now she knew why. The Anne of 1605 was not like the Anne of 1588 – the grey eyes back then seemed to sparkle more with pleasure than piety, and the dark ringlets that had once hung loose around her face were now silver-grey and held neatly within her black headdress. Yet she was, without doubt, the same woman.

For young Richard and Alice, the picture in the locket had made their mother real to them. They could imagine her as a living person rather than the semi-divine creature of their imaginations. And this raised a difficult question – why had this beautiful lady abandoned them? Richard believed she had genuinely loved them and been forced by circumstances to give them up; but Alice found this idea hard to understand or accept, and as she grew older, she began to despise the woman for her callousness.

'Tell me first why you abandoned your children,' Alice said to Anne, not able any longer to disguise the profound bitterness she felt.

Anne raised her eyebrows in surprise. 'I sense you were a foundling, too,' she said. 'And you feel angry at your mother.'

Alice couldn't reply.

'I don't blame you,' said Anne. 'Do you remember her? … I don't suppose you do.'

'Just tell me,' said Alice.

Anne switched her gaze to Henry, and smiled fondly. 'He won't hear us. While he's praying, he only has ears for God.' She seemed stronger now, more certain of herself. Turning to Alice, she sniffed a little, dried her eyes, and said: 'Very well my dear, I'll tell you why I gave up my children to the orphanage. It was because if I had kept them, their father would have found out about it, and I know for certain he would have given up everything, his whole life, to care for us. I couldn't do that to him. Already there were rumours about him and me when I fell pregnant. If anyone had found out about my condition, it would have destroyed his career in the Church. So I ran away and bore our son in secret…'

Anne paused, and Alice was about to urge her to continue when she noticed her staring apprehensively across the room at Father Henry. He had by now turned from the wall and was gazing back at her, his expression full of wonder and curiosity, as if he was seeing her for the first time. He came over then and knelt before her, taking both of her hands in his.

'Not only God, Anne,' he said.

'What?' she breathed.

'You said, when I prayed I only have ears for God. Well, that's not always so.'

'You've been listening…'

'Is that why you disappeared from me all those years ago?' he asked.

Alice stared at him, dumbstruck. Father Henry was… *her father?*

'Aye,' said Anne.

'You broke my heart,' he told her. 'I would have given it all up…'

'I know. And I pray that you can find it in your heart to forgive me. It may help to reflect on what you have become – all the people you've comforted, all the lives you've saved. None of that would have been possible had we followed our desires…'

Henry continued to stare at her, unblinking. 'And when you came back that night a year and a half later?'

'I missed you,' she said, her eyes melting again. 'I couldn't bear to be apart from you.'

'And yet the next day you went away again.'

'My little boy needed me,' Anne said. 'But that visit, however brief, had its consequences. I fell pregnant again, and this time I had a daughter.'

Henry gripped her hands hard. He too had begun to cry.

'Forgive me,' she sobbed.

Alice watched as her parents embraced. So many competing emotions were fighting within her, it was hard to know how to feel. *Henry was her father!* And it turned out Anne hadn't behaved callously in leaving them on the steps of the orphanage – it had been an act of selfless love, a noble sacrifice, to save Henry's career. At least that was how Anne explained it. But was that true? Alice wanted to believe it, yet a worm of doubt still gnawed at her.

'Mistress?' she said.

Anne raised her head from Henry's chest. 'What is it, my dear?'

'You gave up your children to the orphanage so that Father Henry could pursue his vocation as a priest. But maybe you also did it because your friendship with a Jesuit priest helped strengthen your own status as a leader of the English Catholics. You knew that if you'd told Father Henry you were pregnant, he'd have insisted on giving up his vocation and marrying you, and the life you'd wanted for yourself would never have happened. So your children were an inconvenience to you as much as to Father Henry, if not more. That was why you had to get rid of them…'

Anne heard all this without complaint or protest, but Henry had begun shaking his head long before Alice had finished speaking. 'You have it all wrong, child,' he said. 'Anne would have been a leading light of our community with or without me. When I first met her, she was already a brilliant hostess, organising prayer meetings and fundraising events to help pay the recusancy fines of the poorer members of our flock. She was instrumental in helping me at the start of my career. Any success I have had I owe to her.'

'You are far too modest as always, Henry,' said Anne, '– but Alice is right in one sense. I did not give enough consideration at the time to the fate of my children, of *our* children. It was only later that I began to realise how much joy I had denied, not only to myself but to them, and also to you, dear Henry – the joy of being a parent, but also the joy of being a child beloved by parents. For many years now I have lived with the awareness of all the joy I have denied by my cruel act of abandonment, and this awareness torments me. It doesn't stop or fade with time – if anything, it grows stronger by the day.'

'Then let it stop now!' cried Alice, who had heard enough to satisfy her. She reached inside her tunic and pulled out the locket.

As soon as Anne set eyes on the ornately engraved silver case, she let out a cry of shock. Her mouth open, she raised her eyes to Alice, and said: 'My girl. Y-You're my little girl.'

'Mama,' wept Alice, and they fell into each other's arms.

After immersing herself for some time in the soft eglantine scent of her mother, Alice remembered Henry and shyly turned to him. 'Father?'

Henry smiled. 'In both senses of the word, so it seems,' he said, and put his arms around Alice and Anne.

When Anne could speak again, she asked after her son.

'You will meet him soon,' said Alice.

'Ah, praise God, he is alive too! What's his name?'

'Richard.'

Anne seemed lost, dizzy almost, with happiness. 'You know I had a feeling about you, the moment we met,' she said. 'I felt a profound connection. And when you said you grew up in the same orphanage, I could barely contain my excitement. Perhaps that explains the depth of my anger when I thought you'd deceived me. I cannot tell you what a raw nerve you touched…'

'It has been an extraordinary day,' said Henry. 'First we are taken here as prisoners in fear of our lives, and then I discover I have a family with the woman I have always loved.' His eyes were red with sorrow. 'But I cannot help a feeling of regret…'

'Don't,' said Anne, tenderly wiping a tear from his cheek. 'Let's not dwell on what might have been. Let's celebrate today, and the arrival of our daughter, this unexpected gift from God.'

Chapter 27

The Last Stand

HOLBECHE HOUSE, 7TH NOVEMBER 1605

T he three of them talked on for a while. Anne was eager to hear more about her lost children's lives and how they had ended up as players and spies. So Alice told them a version of their story that she hoped wouldn't shock or upset her parents too much.

'You keep mentioning this young man, Tom,' observed Henry at one point.

'Do I?' said Alice, surprised.

'Is he important to you?' asked Anne.

'He's a good friend,' said Alice, keeping her face and

voice neutral. 'He helped me when Richard disappeared.'

'I hope we can meet him one day,' said Anne.

Alice was about to reply when she heard voices muttering on the other side of the door. She rose to her feet and went closer to the door.

'The Sheriff of Worcester is coming, John,' one of the guards was saying. 'Just now, from the attic window I spotted his banners approaching through the forest. He'll be here within the hour. We should leave now, find another hideout, live to fight another day. Are you with me?'

'Catesby ordered us to stay put,' said another voice. 'We have plenty of weapons. We can hold out.'

Footsteps approached, and then she heard Catesby's voice, sounding cheerful: 'Good news, my friends. The enemy has fallen for our ploy. Robert Wintour rode out and let himself be captured by the Sheriff. He told him they'll find nothing here at Holbeche – that we're all holed up at Bradenstoke, and now the Sheriff and his men are riding with all speed for Warwickshire.'

Catesby's cackles faded as he walked off down the corridor.

We have to act! thought Alice desperately. Somehow they had to attract the attention of the royal forces before they got too far away.

She waited until she heard one of the guards leave, then she knocked urgently on the door.

'What is it?' said the one she knew of as John.

'We need help!' called Alice. 'Father Henry is sick!'

She mimed to Henry to start acting unwell, and he attempted a series of loud coughs.

'Alright, alright,' said John.

Alice heard the key turning in the lock, and she tensed, ready to spring into action. As soon as the door opened, she flew at him and punched him hard in the jaw. John fell back in surprise. Before he could recover, Alice tugged the sword from his belt, and held it, two-handed before her, the tip aimed at his chest. John looked furious, but too overawed to fight back – at least for now. Instead, he resorted to taunts: 'What will you do now then?' he sneered at her. 'There are guards front and back. You'll never escape.'

'I'm not planning to escape,' Alice told him.

He laughed.

'I'm glad you find me amusing,' said Alice. 'That's the first step to becoming a friend.'

'Indeed,' he smiled, his hand inching towards the other weapon in his belt – a dagger.

'And if we're friends, we ought to trust each other,' said Alice.

'On that we are agreed,' said John.

'So I feel I must apologise.'

'Apologise for what?' frowned John. His hand had by now grasped the handle of the dagger and he was slowly drawing it out.

'For this,' said Alice, and she whacked him hard over the side of the head with his sword. John collapsed. Looking down at the unconscious figure, she sighed: 'Not the action of a friend, I know.'

Henry and Anne were by now on their feet, gazing at her with awe and respect. Alice left the cell and entered the armoury next door. She counted the gunpowder barrels. There were six in all. *Enough for a big bang!* After checking no other guards were about, she raised her sword above one of the barrels and plunged its point into the top. 'Help me with this, Father,' she said – and they both smiled at the double meaning of the word. *Would this become a family joke?* she wondered.

Between them, Henry and Alice lifted the barrel and, at her instruction, allowed some of its black powder to trickle out. Slowly, they began moving towards the doorway at the far end of the armoury while the powder continued to pour from the barrel so that it formed a narrow line along the floor.

'Do you mind me asking why we're doing this?' asked Henry.

'We're creating a fuse,' said Alice. 'We need to attract the attention of the Sheriff of Worcester before he gets too far away. I should think six barrels of gunpowder ought to do it.'

'What about your new friend?' asked Anne, looking at the unconscious John.

'We'll drag him to safety, don't worry,' Alice said over her shoulder.

When they reached the door, they peered out into the lobby. It was empty, but Alice could hear the plotters arguing in the next-door room. Leaving one hand beneath the barrel, she put a finger to her lips to signal the need for quiet. Then she and Henry passed through the door and proceeded to sprinkle the line of gunpowder across the lobby's black-and-white tiled floor.

They extended the fuse as far as the threshold of the front door, before returning, with the barrel, to the armoury. Alice grabbed some matches from a shelf and put them in her pocket while Anne and Henry hauled the inert John through the lobby and out of the house, depositing him behind a stone well in the middle of the forecourt.

Back in the lobby, Alice lit one of the matches in the flame of a wall lamp, then returned to the threshold and held it above the end of the fuse.

Henry came and crouched close to her. 'Being a player on the stage, I expect you've had some experience of explosives,' he whispered.

She nodded sagely. 'Aye.'

'So you've worked with gunpowder before?'

'Not as such,' she admitted.

'You know, for example, how long we have before it explodes, and how big the explosion will be? Will those men in that room be killed, for example, or the princess upstairs? And where precisely should we place ourselves to be safe?'

Alice furrowed her brow at him. She didn't know the answer to any of these questions – all of them quite legitimate.

She had acted impulsively, and now she didn't know what to do.

While she was struggling with this dilemma, the door to the next-door room suddenly swung open and Catesby came striding out. He stared at Alice, then at the long trail of gunpowder, and emitted a great roar of rage.

In a fright, Alice dropped the lit match, and it fell onto the fuse. A flashing, sparkling, scorchingly bright flame began dancing and crackling along the floor at astonishing speed. Within seconds it had reached the far side of the lobby and had disappeared through the door into the armoury.

'Run!' screamed Alice. 'Run! Run! Run!'

She, Henry and Anne sprinted away from the house as a series of huge, deafening cracks split the air. She heard shattering glass and crumbling masonry behind her, and felt a hot blast of air that knocked her to the ground.

When she came to, seconds later, she had a taste of earth in her mouth, and her ears buzzed and rang. Shakily, she climbed out of the ornamental flower bed where she'd landed and got to her feet.

Holbeche House – at least the front part – looked intact, except for the windows, every one of which was smashed. A big pall of black smoke was rising into the sky from the rear of the house. Alice ran over to Anne and Henry and helped them to their feet. They looked bruised but unhurt.

Just then a crazed-looking figure came staggering out of the house. His clothes were smoking, his face black with soot, his hair and beard singed grey. From the charred hook at the end of his burnt sleeve, Alice realised it was Catesby.

'You!' he bellowed at Alice. 'I'll kill you for this!'

More of the conspirators began stumbling out of the front entrance, coughing from the smoke and dazed from the force of the explosion. The princess emerged last, her dress begrimed, her hair in disarray.

'What shall we do now?' groaned Tresham.

'We should leave before they get here!' cried someone. 'The armoury is destroyed, along with all the weapons. Our only chance is to flee.'

'We stay and fight say I!' growled Guido Fawkes. 'We still have the weapons we carry. I'll personally kill any man who runs!'

Alice signalled to Henry and Anne, and the three began backing away through the garden. They clambered over a wall and ran into the surrounding woods. Taking shelter behind a stout oak, they looked back towards Holbeche to see several of the conspirators still milling about on the forecourt in a state of shock. Tresham was sitting on the ground openly weeping. Fawkes and Catesby were giving orders, but no one appeared to be listening. There were arguments, mutinous mutterings, and no one noticed as the diminutive figure of Princess Elizabeth began wandering away from the house, shambling down the driveway and through the gate.

When she reached the road, Alice ran to her and led her by the hand back to the tree where she, Anne and Henry were hiding out. 'You'll be safe with us, Your Majesty. Help is on the way.'

'I want my brother Henry,' Elizabeth whimpered.

Within half an hour, they heard a blare of trumpets from further down the road. The Sheriff of Worcester was coming.

This prospect brought, at long last, a semblance of discipline and purpose to the conspirators. They lit the cords on their matchlocks and took cover in the front room bays amid the shattered window glass.

Worcester's mounted forces – knights and men-at-arms – soon galloped into view. They were followed by infantry – pikemen, archers and arquebusiers, who fanned out to surround the house. As they did so, gunfire erupted from the front windows, and this was answered by a barrage of arrows and artillery from Worcester's men.

The battle was loud, violent, and brief. After ten minutes, the house fell silent as the conspirators ran out of ammunition. A white rag was draped from one of the windows, and a little later the surviving members of the Gunpowder Plot came limping out of the front door. They carried with them the bodies of comrades killed in the final shoot-out, among them Robert Catesby. The survivors were shackled and escorted into an iron-barred prisoner wagon.

At this point, Alice, Anne and Henry emerged from

their hiding-place and escorted Princess Elizabeth to the Sheriff. He was shocked to find the king's daughter here, especially in her bedraggled state – for news had yet to reach him of her abduction. When Alice explained their story to him, he thanked her for her gallant actions and confirmed it had been the explosion and resulting cloud of black smoke that had prompted his decision to return to Holbeche House.

Epilogue

WHITEHALL PALACE, 26TH JANUARY 1606

he King's Men's debut performance of *Macbeth* was an enormous success, with many describing it as Shakespeare's greatest work since *Hamlet*. The crowd at the Globe loved the play for its violence and murder. They were both delighted and terrified by the witches, the ghost of Banquo and the vision of a floating dagger. One audience member swore the play was cursed, and that its script contained magic spells that would doom all those who uttered them for ever more.

Richard Burbage, playing Macbeth, was tough, impassioned and tormented by ambition – those 'black and deep desires'. As for Alice's Lady Macbeth, few could remember a more evil and manipulative female character in any drama. A week later, when they presented the same play at Whitehall Palace, the king himself approached Alice afterwards to offer his congratulations on her performance. She decided it might be best not to tell him that it had been inspired by his nine-year-old daughter.

King James was genuinely thrilled by the play, especially the portrayal of his ancestor Duncan as a wise and noble ruler, 'his silver skin laced with his golden blood'. He also appreciated the way Shakespeare had woven in references to the recent Gunpowder Plot. For example, when Lady Macbeth tells her husband to 'look like an innocent flower, but be the serpent under it', it called to mind the medal James had ordered to commemorate the foiling of the plot, which portrayed a snake hiding among flowers.

Lord Cecil added his own congratulations to the king's, telling the playwright: 'I challenged you to prove your loyalty, Mr Shakespeare, and you have done so in style. Never have I seen a more nightmarish depiction of the calamities that ensue when a divinely appointed monarch is murdered. Papists should take note! Yet there is one aspect of all this that puzzles me. In Richard Fletcher's report on the Powder Treason, he stated that Francis Tresham burned the manuscript of this play during a banquet at Rushton Hall. If that is true, then how were you able to put it on for us today?'

'I am very careful with my manuscripts, sire,' revealed Will, 'and would never leave them out on tables near windows. I suspected Tresham might be after it, so I left a fake one on the table for him to steal, while keeping the real one safe in a trunk beneath my bed.'

'I greatly admire that kind of thinking,' said Cecil. 'If you ever consider putting down your quill, I'm sure I could offer you a fine career in His Majesty's Secret Service.'

'The reports he'd pen might be something special,' smiled John Heminges.

'Did I hear you mention Rushton Hall, sire?' said Gus, bustling up to Cecil. 'If it is of interest to you, I have plenty of information on the conspirators, gathered during my captivity there.'

'It's quite alright, Mr Philips,' said Cecil. 'All the men involved in the plot are now dead. Catesby was killed in the shoot-out at Holbeche House, Fawkes was executed, and Tresham died during his imprisonment in the Tower. The heads of all three traitors are now displayed for all to see on London Bridge.'

'A fitting end for those vicious men, sire,' said Gus with a shudder. 'That Mr Tresham would kill you for no reason at all. Even talking could get you murdered.'

'It must have been especially dangerous for you then,' said Cecil.

The audience at Whitehall Palace that day included Mistress Anne Vaux. Although Cecil had expressed his aversion to the idea of inviting such a prominent recusant, Alice persuaded him that it was important to her. 'She proved her loyalty during the Gunpowder affair,' she said. 'And hers is a moderate voice within the Catholic community that ought to be rewarded.' Of course Alice's real relationship to Anne could never be publicly acknowledged, but that didn't stop them from seeing each other. Indeed, both Alice and Richard had visited their parents at Whitewebbs on three occasions over the previous two months. Richard, overwhelmed by the news that his parents had been found, had cried on first meeting them. He recalled his mother's silver crucifix, her scent of sweet briar, and the way she sang 'Greensleeves', all of which filled him with an intense yet soothing nostalgia. And he fell in love with the wild garden at Whitewebbs, sharing Anne's love of untamed nature.

After the performance at Whitehall Palace, Anne took her children's hands in hers and and gave them a squeeze. 'I'm not going to cry,' she said to them. 'I promised Henry I wouldn't cry. But I just wanted to say, I'm so proud of both of you. And so is Henry. If someone had said to me, when I left you both on the steps of that orphanage all those years ago, that one day you'd grow up to be spies keeping this country safe, a–and perform plays before the king, I j-just…'

Alice offered her mother a handkerchief as the tears began to flow.

In another part of the room, sweating near a rather-too-hot fireplace, stood Tom and Sir Francis Bacon.

'Did you enjoy the play, sir?' Tom asked.

'Aye,' said his distracted master. He was sniffing the leg of a chicken he had picked up from a table laden with food. 'This meat doesn't smell too good,' he muttered.

'Best not to eat it then, sir,' said Tom.

'It's this overheated palace,' said Sir Francis. 'Turns the meat bad.' He gazed out of the window at the snowflakes falling in the courtyard, and a bright glow began to spread across his face.

Tom guessed what was coming.

'I have had an idea,' said Sir Francis.

'Never, sir! Really?'

Sir Francis was too engrossed in his own thoughts to notice the sarcasm. 'Refrigeration, Tom,' he declared. 'We can preserve meat by packing it with snow.'

'And what happens when there's no snow about, sir?'

The philosopher nodded bleakly. 'Aye, Tom. You have put your finger on a potential flaw in my proposal. That, as I have discovered over the years of our acquaintance, is your most important talent.'

Later that day, Tom, Alice and Richard took a walk along the banks of the river, heading south from Whitehall Palace. Sunlight glistened on the snow that frosted the quays and jetties, and twinkled like polished stone on the grey waters.

'You were both brilliant today,' said Tom.

'*Alice* was brilliant,' said Richard. 'I was ordinary. As Macduff's son, I had just one scene, before getting murdered by Macbeth's thugs.'

'You were cute and clever,' said Alice. 'And then, all too quickly, you were dead. It was the most brutal moment in the play. And that was down to your performance.'

'You are too kind, sister.'

They walked on a while in silence, their breath visible as little clouds before their faces. Ahead of them loomed the Gothic spires of the Abbey, and the long pitched roof of Westminster Hall, now covered in thick snow like a giant marzipan cake. As they passed the venerable landmarks of the Palace of Westminster, the same thought struck all of them: these buildings were still standing today, thanks almost entirely to their efforts.

'What will become of us?' Tom wondered.

'You will be a world-renowned natural philosopher,' predicted Alice. 'As for Richard and I, we shall continue getting heckled and spat on by the groundlings at the Globe until we are at least as old as John Heminges.'

'Or else we'll die an early death, courtesy of the Beagle,' muttered Richard.

'A more likely fate, I agree,' said Alice.

'In that case, we should live for today,' said Tom, 'and spare no thought for the morrow.'

'That is a most excellent philosophy,' said Richard.

'Where are you going?' asked Tom, as Richard began striking out upon a westward path, taking him away from the river.

'Living for today!' called Richard. 'Gus has given us the rest of the day off, and I intend to spend it over there.' He pointed towards a snowbound meadow, beyond which lay a misty blue line of trees.

'What is that place?' asked Alice.

'Hyde Park,' said Richard. 'It's a royal hunting ground, and not open to the public. But I know how to hide from the rangers. What's important is that it's forest, and at this moment there's no place I'd rather be.'

Alice and Tom bade him farewell, and continued on their southward route along the river bank.

'I suppose you must be getting back to Sir Francis soon,' said Alice.

'Oh, he'll be too busy messing around with chickens and snow to worry about me,' said Tom. '… It's his latest idea,' he added, by way of explanation.

'Chickens and snow, eh?' She laughed.

They stopped and leaned upon a fence, watching the paddles of a giant watermill slowly turning in the current of the river. Beneath them, wading birds pecked at shellfish in the muddy shallows.

'The sun is quite beautiful on the river, don't you think?' observed Alice.

Live for today, Tom was thinking. And: *if I do this, it will be the bravest thing I've ever done.*

Alice shivered in a sudden breeze, and Tom moved

a step closer to her. *Alice or Ophelia? He didn't care any more who she was…*

As she watched the pretty patterns of the sunlight on the surface of the water, she thought to herself: *why is my heart beating so loudly?* Then, all of a sudden, she felt his arm around her waist and his lips pressing down upon hers.

Inside she began to smile.

A clatter of horse hooves broke their idyll. It was followed by the swish and screech of wheels sliding to a stop on the icy road. Alice and Tom broke away from each other and turned around.

A gilded carriage bearing the royal coat of arms had drawn up beside them as a liveried footman leapt down to open the door. The sole occupant, Lord Cecil, leaned out and beckoned to them. If he'd seen what they'd been up to, he showed no sign of it.

'Get in! Get in!' he cried. 'I need you both to come to the Palace this instant. My agents have intercepted a suspicious message, and I fear a new plot is brewing. Now where the devil is Richard…?'

Tom and Alice smiled ruefully at each other. 'Here we go again,' she whispered, and he reached out and squeezed her hand one last time before they climbed inside the carriage.

The End

A selected list of Scribo titles

Gladiator School by Dan Scott

1	Blood Oath	978-1-908177-48-3	£6.99
2	Blood & Fire	978-1-908973-60-3	£6.99
3	Blood & Sand	978-1-909645-16-5	£6.99
4	Blood Vengeance	978-1-909645-62-2	£6.99
5	Blood & Thunder	978-1-910184-20-2	£6.99
6	Blood Justice	978-1-910184-43-1	£6.99

Iron Sky by Alex Woolf

1	Dread Eagle	978-1-909645-00-4	£9.99
2	Call of the Phoenix	978-1-910184-87-5	£6.99

Children of the Nile by Alain Surget

1	Cleopatra must be Saved!	978-1-907184-73-4	£5.99
2	Caesar, Who's he?	978-1-907184-74-1	£5.99
3	Prisoners in the Pyramid	978-1-909645-59-2	£5.99
4	Danger at the Circus!	978-1-909645-60-8	£5.99

Ballet School by Fiona Macdonald

1	Peter & The Wolf	978-1-911242-37-6	£6.99
2	Samira's Garden	978-1-912006-62-5	£6.99

Aldo Moon by Alex Woolf

1 Aldo Moon and the Ghost
  at Gravewood Hall   978-1-908177-84-1 £6.99

The Shakespeare Plot by Alex Woolf

1 Assassin's Code   978-1-911242-38-3 £9.99
2 The Dark Forest   978-1-912006-95-3 £9.99
3 The Powder Treason   978-1-912006-33-5 £9.99

Visit our website at:

www.salariya.com

All Scribo and Salariya Book Company titles can be
ordered from your local bookshop, or by post from:

The Salariya Book Co. Ltd,
25 Marlborough Place
Brighton BN1 1UB